"Guess who's been invited to take Ron's advanced ballet class?"

"Peter!" I jump up and clap my hands. I once heard Madam Dukowsky say that dancing is in Peter's blood. And when I watch him in class, I sometimes think he was *born* dancing. He doesn't seem to be struggling like the rest of us. There's something special about Peter, all right, and it's no secret that he is every teacher's favorite. I'm sure he'll be a star one day.

"Don't tell anyone, okay?" he is saying.

"If *I* were invited to take advanced, I'd be shouting it from the rooftops," I answer. "It's a good thing I like you, Peter, or I could easily hate you for being so good."

MAYBE NEXT YEAR . . .

"Fluent style, strong characterization and dialogue."
—*The Bulletin of the Center for Children's Books*
(recommended)

Maybe Next Year . . .

Amy Hest

A BANTAM SKYLARK BOOK®
TORONTO • NEW YORK • LONDON • SYDNEY • AUCKLAND

RL 5, IL age 9 and up

MAYBE NEXT YEAR . . .

A Bantam Book / published by arrangement with
Clarion Books

PRINTING HISTORY

Clarion Books edition published October 1982
Bantam Starfire edition / April 1985
Bantam Skylark edition / January 1989

Skylark Books is a registered trademark of Bantam Books, a division of
Bantam Doubleday Dell Publishing Group, Inc. Registered in U.S. Patent
and Trademark Office and elsewhere.

ISBN 0-553-15652-7

Published simultaneously in the United States and Canada

Bantam Books are published by Bantam Books, a division of Bantam
Doubleday Dell Publishing Group, Inc. Its trademark, consisting of the words
"Bantam Books" and the portrayal of a rooster, is Registered in U.S. Patent
and Trademark Office and in other countries. Marca Registrada. Bantam
Books, 666 Fifth Avenue, New York, New York 10103.

PRINTED IN THE UNITED STATES OF AMERICA

O   0 9 8 7 6 5 4 3 2 1

For Frieda
of course

1

"I never asked to be born," I mutter. Cross-legged on my bed, I am busy snipping little pieces of thread from the new ballet slippers. Yanking the elastic to be sure it is fastened well to each pink shoe, I lean over to study my face in the mirror on the low white dresser. Pale. I am winter pale.

"Kate!" There she goes again.

Like the beautiful leading ladies in those old Bogart movies, I silently open the top dresser drawer. My fingers fly across rolled socks and Nana's antique camisole. I pull out the precious compact ("waltzflower red," the smiling Woolworth's salesgirl had insisted) and give my cheeks a "subtle dusting," just the way she had demonstrated last Monday in her high swivel chair.

I have good reason for keeping the little compact undercover, and it's not because I'm a particularly sneaky person. It's just that my grandmother is not exactly the type to pat me on the head and say, "Of course, dear, you go ahead and buy all the makeup you want." Besides, she has a peculiar way of knowing when you're up to something, and worst of all is when you *know* she knows, even though she doesn't say a word about it. The walls have eyes, she teases. Or is it ears?

Even now, there's something foxy about the way she stands there in the dim of the living room, her hands on either hip. "Thank you, Kate," she says, very down-to-business. "Hurry. It's getting dark and the *Shabbas* won't wait, even for a ballerina."

One thing's for sure: You don't argue with Jessie Stein. Of course you're entitled to complain a little, but mostly you do what she says, or pay with the guilt of knowing you have hurt or failed her.

"Don't forget," she says as I back into my red ski parka, "Pinky is waiting for you at the station."

"Okay."

She hands me a starched dollar bill. "This is for the *challah*," she reminds me. "Now, hurry!"

"I am. I'm hurrying." I bend slightly to kiss her crinkly-soft cheek. "Will you look at this," I tease. "Even in sneakers I'm taller than my own grandmother!"

"You're going to be tall and skinny," she answers, "like your father."

"Cross your fingers." I twirl past her and out the front door.

Outside, the wind snaps around the corner. All

winter long it whooshes off the Hudson River and funnels cold air up our block. Now I hold my arms out stiff and let it push me toward Broadway.

We live in one of those grand old buildings on Riverside Drive in Manhattan. It was built ages ago, in the 1920s, I think. Nana is very proud to live here and constantly says things like, "They just don't make buildings like this anymore." She's talking about the marble walls in the lobby and apartments with big rooms and fancy molding on the ceilings. Some apartments even have fireplaces. I wish we did; they're so romantic.

Nana loves to tell us how different the Drive *used* to be, when she and Grampa first moved here. "Elegant and chic," she insists, "just like Fifth Avenue." To tell the truth, I like Riverside Drive a lot better than snooty Fifth Avenue. I love the quiet of it and the way it winds and curves and hugs Riverside Park. The Hudson River is on the far side of the park, and even though people complain that it's dirty and polluted, it happens to look very pretty. If you live in the right apartment, you get a great view. I'm sorry to say we live in back. No river. No park. No view.

From several blocks away the bells of the Cathedral of St. John the Divine remind me not to dawdle. "Sundown is at 4:45," Nana warned. I start to run.

Splats of water make long, wiggly trails on the door of Mother's Best Bakery. I push it open and the chubby gray-haired woman on the other side of the counter smiles at me. "Afternoon, Kate." Her cheeks are painted Kewpie doll pink and I am tempted to tell her about the free demonstrations at Woolworth's. *"Challah,* dear?" she asks.

"Thank you, Mrs. Muller." I try to smile when she hands me the warm waxed bag, then a small buttery cookie. The cookie business is all right when nobody is around, but I die if there is. I'm much too old for that sort of thing.

"Regards to your grandmother," Mrs. Muller calls after me.

I am waiting for Pinky (short for Elizabeth Pincus Newman) at the entrance to the subway station at 110th Street and Broadway. I am freezing and she is late. Holding the bread to my chest, I hop from one foot to the other. Left. Right. Left, right, left. The streetlights blink on. Bunches of commuters trudge up subway stairs, then scatter in a hundred directions. I eat the cookie to keep from being furious with my sister. Also, I am trying hard not to think about my furry boots, warm and snug—and under my bed.

"Kate!" It's Pinky at last, waving her arm around as if she hadn't seen me in a week.

Pinky will be ten next June, and I turned twelve in October. I'm sensible enough to know it isn't the worst thing in the world to have a little sister, but it isn't the best thing either. I can't even say there's anything specifically wrong with Pinky. It's just this feeling I have that she's always *there*.

Sisters are supposed to at least resemble each other, but Pinky and I don't look at all alike. First of all, I've heard people call her adorable. I don't happen to think she's so adorable but I can see why they might say it. She's got one of those babyish turned-up noses, with freckles. (Mine is straight and plain, "strong," Nana says.) Her hair makes chestnut-colored curlicues that bounce off her ears when she walks. Mine is long, no curls, and I fix a braid if there's time. Ariane Dukowsky, this very opinionated girl at my ballet school, once called my hair dishwater blond. Nana just calls it blond, no adjectives.)

"We're late," I announce.

"Wait!" Pinky is doing this combination run-skip-skip, run-skip-skip alongside me. Her green rubber boots are clumsy and a nylon book bag keeps slipping off her shoulder. "I need to talk to you."

"I'm listening." We turn west at 109th Street, Nana's Sabbath sun is threateningly low in the sky. I reach for Pinky's hand and run with her to the end of the block.

"I'm in big trouble," she pants. "Nana's going to kill me."

I do three *grands jetés* across the quiet marbled lobby. "She isn't the killing type," I answer.

Our elevator has a way of never being around when you need it, like when you're late. Like now. So we head for the back stairs and I take them two at a time.

"Miss Falk says no more piano lessons," Pinky

reports from the bottom step. "She says it isn't fair to waste her time and Nana's money."

"Again?" I press my tongue to the roof of my mouth, then let it click noisily.

"She's going to phone Nana," Pinky sighs. "Tonight."

"Well, you're right about one thing," I say. "Nana *is* going to kill you."

Even from the stairwell you know it's Friday night. I close my eyes and inhale the warmth—the chicken and chicken soup, baked candied sweet potatoes, Nana's scrumptious noodle *kugel*.

Apartment 3C. The door swings open and my grandmother greets us. "It's time!" she says, turning on her heel. We drop our jackets and mittens in a heap on the faded blue club chair, then follow her toward the kitchen.

"Kate," Nana says without even looking at me, "your hair is wild. Please tie it off your face." She is standing at the stove, her back to us. "How was the lesson, Pinky?"

Pinky nudges my arm. Her brown eyes say we mustn't talk piano. I silently agree to help her, this time.

"Mmmmmm." I lift the cover off Nana's old aluminum pot and watch the carrots and greens swish around in a whirlpool of chicken soup. "When is supper?"

"I'm ready!" My grandmother seems to fly toward me.

As it is every Friday night, the kitchen table is set with our good silver. It's got squiggles and scallopy edges and in my opinion is plain ugly. But Nana makes a big deal about polishing it once a week so it may take a proper place on the Sabbath table, along with the lacy white tablecloth she says is from her trousseau.

Now she carefully fills three narrow glasses about halfway each with the sweet maroon wine. Quite suddenly we shift into a kind of Sabbath calm. Nana unties her flowery apron and hangs it across the back of her chair. For the prayer she covers her head with a square of black cloth, which is always so striking against her white hair.

My grandmother may not be the prettiest woman in New York City, or the most glamorous, but she's got the softest fluff of hair I've ever seen. Every month I trim it over the bathroom sink. We drape a raggy old bath towel around her shoulders and she squirms like a two-year-old if I take more than five minutes. "Looking beautiful takes time," I try to tell her, but she doesn't pay attention.

How nice she looks tonight, in her creamy silk blouse, the same one every week, and the black skirt with pleats. I glance down at my own worn jeans and promise myself to be prettier next week, more special for Friday night. For Nana. And some- how for Grampa, too. Even though Grampa died nearly two years ago, it seems like only last week he was sitting here with us, bragging to Nana, "You are most beautiful of all on the *Shabbas*, Jessie dear."

"Ach, hush!" Shaking her head, Nana would flush—as if Grampa's words were not intended for little girls' ears.

Two white candles stand in polished brass holders. Nana lights each one. Then, in slow, lulling movements, she circles the small flames, waving her arms around and around. The candles sputter, and flicker, but will burn on for hours. Nana's eyes are closed, yet her lips are rippling—up, down, up and down—mumbling Hebrew words I can't understand.

When finally she looks up, her lashes are wet, but she smiles. "Good *Shabbas*, my darlings." She kisses Pinky's forehead and mine.

"Good *Shabbas*, Nana."

Every week it's the same. I get this vague pit-in-the-stomach feeling as I watch my grandmother perform the age-old ritual. All week long she loves us and laughs with us, she scolds and bosses. But these few minutes belong to her alone. She shuts her eyes and somehow drifts off, to a time or place that has nothing to do with Pinky and me. I hold my breath and wait for her sweet return.

Once, when I was seven or eight, I asked Nana why the Sabbath candles made her sad. "I cry for our bad times and the good," she told me. "Every day I seem to miss your parents a little more than the day before. I gave birth to your mother, Kate, but your father was like my own son. We were very close," she said quietly.

My mother and father died a long time ago, when I was four. People say I was too young to remember the accident, but I do. In those days my parents took us to the seashore every summer. We rented a little white cottage on the beach and the four of us slept in one room.

One day we were picnicking on a chartered boat. The rest happened very fast—the explosion and fire. Then the horrible screaming. They say we were all taken to a hospital, but I don't remember that part.

Afterward Pinky and I came to live with Nana and Grampa on Riverside Drive. They seemed so sad to me, and old. For a long time I used to believe, or pretend to believe, my parents would come back. But of course they didn't. Every year, right before Christmas, Nana sends off a big package to a fisherman in Nova Scotia, Canada, whom she's never met. He's the one who saved Pinky and me. I wish he could have saved my parents, too.

"Stop slurping, Pinky," Nana is saying. "By the way, how did the little Brahms piece go this afternoon?"

My sister takes a sudden interest in the goings-on at the bottom of her soup bowl. She appears, in fact, not to hear Nana.

"Where is Mr. Schumacher tonight?" I ask casually.

"He's working late," Nana answers, "winding up some big corporate deal." Mr. Schumacher is an old-time neighbor of ours and Nana says he's a very important lawyer. He lives upstairs in 14A, alone now, so we invite him to dinner a lot, especially on Fridays.

"He sure works hard," I comment.

Nana looks at Pinky across the round table. "The Brahms?" she asks simply.

Pinky sighs quietly, as if she were going to confess, and I try one more time. "Nana," I begin, "I need to talk to you about a new leotard. The blue one is getting tight, you know, in the bosom department."

"I see," she answers, "so you're getting a little bosom in the bosom department."

"It's true!" Pinky exclaims. "I saw it."

You quit spying on me! I want to shout, but I don't. *Privacy! I need privacy!* I want to shriek, but I don't do that either.

"That's fine news." Nana smiles at me, then turns to Pinky. "So, the Brahms wasn't so hot?"

See what I mean! My grandmother just *knows* these things. I try one last time to change the subject. Perhaps my sister will one day return the favor. "Can I get a new leotard tomorrow?" I ask.

Nana is stacking bowls in the sink when the telephone in the foyer rings. Pinky gets this innocent I-didn't-hear-anything look on her face. And even before I pick up the phone, I know it's Miss Falk.

2

Saturdays are best. I love to get up early and sometimes even set my alarm for seven. Pinky and I share the room, so I have to be extra-quiet if I'm to have any privacy at all. My sister loves to do what I do. Nana says it's to be expected, that Pinky copies because she looks up to me. She says I should be flattered, but I'm not. Sometimes a girl has to be alone.

Right now I'm trying hard not to spill the hot cocoa I've brought back to bed. I fluff two pillows behind my head and lean back, balancing the mug in one hand and a book against my knees. I love to read in bed. My favorite books are about girls who want to be dancers, and I think I've read most of them by now. My special favorite is called *Ballet for Nina* and the copy I have was once my mother's. There's an inscription on the inside cover that says,

"To my darling Deborah. Happy Birthday. With love, Uncle Julius." On page thirty-seven there's a chocolate smudge. It is very faint, but I know it was my mother's because Nana says she had quite a sweet tooth.

When the little red clock between our twin beds says eight o'clock, I leave my cozy nest to practice *glissade, glissade, jeté, pas de bourrée* in front of the long mirror on the inside of the closet door. I glance over at my sister. Sleeping. I take off my pajama top. My breasts are getting bigger now and in winter I wear a bra. Ariane once told me when your breasts are big enough the boys like to squeeze them. She insisted it's a pretty sexy thing to do, but I doubt it.

"Where's your top?" Pinky is leaning on her elbow. Her eyes are focused on the upper portion of my body.

I grab the pajama off the dresser and pull it over my head, wondering why I couldn't be lucky enough to have a room of my own. "How come you're up so early?" I demand.

Pinky drops back on her pillow. Very dramatic. "I've made up my mind," she says. "The only solution is for me to run away from home."

"You sound brilliant." I stretch my arms way up, then fold over at the waist so the tip of my nose rests on my knees. "Nana's just angry about the lessons."

Although last night's call from Pinky's piano teacher interrupted the spirit of our dinner, it was not exactly the calamity she is making it out to be. We sat in the kitchen listening to Nana's end of the brief conversation.

Nana: Miss Falk! How are you this evening? [My grandmother may sound innocent but *we* know that she already knows why Miss Falk is calling.]
Pause.
Nana: You're right. Some children are ungrateful.
Pause.
Nana: You're right. Some children are spoiled.
Pause. [This one must last a full minute.]
Nana: You, of course, are the best judge. But I'm sure that a woman with your patience would be willing to give my granddaughter one more chance. For my sake.

When Nana came back to the table, her lips were pulled together in a straight, unfriendly line. She sat down, then folded her hands in front of her. "Pinky," she said quietly, "beginning tonight you will practice one hour every day." My sister opened her mouth, to protest I suppose, but Nana hadn't finished. "You may practice after school, or you may prefer to divide your time—a little in the morning and the rest at night. You work out the details, as long as it's one hour."

"But, Nana . . ."

"Thank you, Pinky." Nana's tone of voice indicated the discussion was over.

One thing about my grandmother is that she's a

pretty stubborn lady. If she gets a notion in her head that one of us ought to be doing something, it's almost impossible to talk her out of it. Like the piano lessons. Pinky did not exactly volunteer to take them. As a matter of fact, she wanted to quit after her first lesson. Nana said to give it time, she would learn to like it.

I happen to know Nana is especially hung up about piano because my mother played when she was a little girl. To this day she claims my mother was so talented she belonged in Carnegie Hall. But there's another side to the story—Grampa's side. *He* used to tell us with those twinkle-blue eyes of his that his daughter, wonderful as she was, had absolutely no ear for music! I have a sneaky suspicion that Grampa's version of this little family history is a shade closer to that long-ago reality.

"Hello. Good morning!" I find Nana poking around the bottom shelf of the refrigerator. She stands up slowly and I kiss her cheek. "Mmmm," I murmur, "your skin is smooth as a baby's."

"Agh," she shakes her head. "I'm two years younger than Central Park, Kate."

"Of course," I answer, "but you happen to have wonderful soft skin. Speaking of babies, Pinky is getting ready to pack a bag."

"Again," she nods. Cracking an egg on the edge of the counter, she lets it plop into a small green bowl.

"Why don't you let her quit piano?" I ask, wondering if Pinky would do such a thing for me.

"We are not quitters." Nana pours some milk into the bowl with the egg, then starts to beat the mixture with a fork. She is wearing her ridiculous gray housedress. Red elephants play ring-around-the-rosy all over it, and it's one of the silliest things I've ever seen.

Two Mother's Days ago Pinky and I bought her a beautiful pale blue morning dress. It has colored ribbons hanging from the shoulders and a stand-up collar. "You're a knockout!" we cheered as we twirled her in front of the full-length mirror in our bedroom.

"Not bad for an old lady." She seemed so pleased with herself, yet she took it off right away, and for reasons I'll never understand, she *saves* it for birthday breakfasts and other special occasions.

"I've been thinking, Nana," I begin slowly. "Wouldn't it be nice if I had my own room? Like the den, for instance. Easy as pie, I could move my stuff in there . . ."

"I've always believed," she cuts in, "that sisters should share a bedroom. It makes them close."

"Sure," I sulk, quite used to her answer.

"Hi." Enter Pinky. Very solemn.

"Morning, Pinky," Nana says cheerfully. "Don't be so glum; it's only an hour a day." She puts a platter of French toast on the table, then gives my sister a hug. "Eat, girls, before it gets cold," she calls to us on her way back to the stove.

One thing about eating in our house is that my grandmother is always jumping up and down during the meal. She runs a jagged race from the kitchen table to the stove, back to the table, the refrigerator, and so on.

"Just once, Jessie Stein, I would like to see you *sit* through an entire meal," Grampa used to complain.

Pinky is now flooding her plate with maple syrup. "That is disgusting," I whisper.

She jabs a tiny piece of toast onto her fork, then drags it through the sweet goo, mumbling, "Mmmm, it tastes so good."

"You are dawdling, Pinky." Nana has the most remarkable way of knowing what's going on at the other end of the room. Our kitchen is divided into two sections. There's the cooking part, which Nana likes to keep clear of noncookers like Pinky and me. She says it's because there's only room for one, but I think she is happiest doing things herself. The eating section is nice. The walls and ceiling are covered with green and white flowery wallpaper, and a tall, narrow window looks out on the same alley you can see from our bedroom.

"I'm going on a diet after breakfast," I announce.

"You need it," Pinky answers sweetly.

"You've got snake hips, Kate. Skinny." Nana helps herself to the single piece of French toast that looks burnt.

"Snake hips or not," I sigh, "I'm the fattest girl in Ballet Three."

"Who wants more French toast?" Nana is back at the stove.

"Me!" says Pinky.

"Me too."

"I thought you're on a diet," Pinky

"Pinky," warns my grandmother, "en emphasizes the *ough*.

It is eleven o'clock by the time I finish packi my dance bag. The navy canvas satchel bulges with leotard and tights, leg warmers, and my pink dance shoes. I fill zippered compartments with a hairbrush and barrettes, extra rubber bands and two chocolate candy bars. For the subway there is always a book in the side pocket.

"So long, Nana. I'm leaving."

"Wear a scarf." She hands me a small brown bag. My grandmother really believes I would drop dead in the middle of class if I weren't fortified with one of her chopped egg sandwiches on whole wheat bread. "Now, enjoy your class," she says. "Be home by five, do you hear?"

"I hear! I hear!" I am already flying down the back stairs.

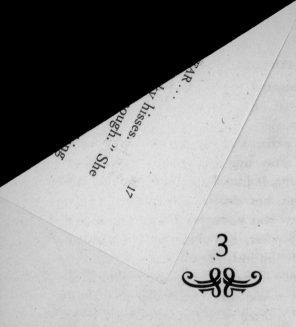

3

The New York Ballet Academy is located in a rickety old building on Eighty-sixth Street and Broadway. I've been studying there since fifth grade. That Christmas Mr. and Mrs. Schumacher took Pinky and me to see *The Nutcracker* at Lincoln Center. I had never been to the ballet before, and the minute the curtain went up on the first act, I was hooked. I remember borrowing a dime from Mrs. Schumacher, and during the intermission I called Nana to ask for lessons. Lucky me, because she said yes. The surprising thing is that Pinky never wanted lessons, too.

"Hey, Kate!" I turn in time to see Peter Robinson dodge a blue city bus in the busy intersection at Eighty-sixth and Broadway.

"You'll kill yourself at that rate," I scold when he is safely at my side. But I'm smiling because it's good to see Peter, especially in one piece.

"Can't," he answers, "can't kill myself until after class."

"Wise guy."

Although I've never had the nerve to tell him, Peter is far and away my best friend. Sure, there are girls from school, like Patricia Mandella and Sabina Moskowitz, but the truth is I'd rather be with Peter. When I was younger, I liked to pretend he was my big brother, but recently I've decided that I'm just a little bit in love with him.

First of all, Peter is the most handsome boy I've ever known. Not movie star handsome, just plain cute. He's a drop shorter than I am, and very thin. His eyes remind me of two aqua almonds, and his hair, a dark shade of auburn, has the nicest way of flopping in his eyes and around his ears, in layers so thick he needs to wear a bandanna during dance class.

"We've got to change your math tutoring day," Peter is saying.

"What's wrong with Wednesdays?" I ask.

Peter has been my algebra coach since October. He tries very hard to make me understand a subject I just can't get a hold on, and even though my grades have improved, they are not exactly terrific.

"Starting next week," Peter answers, "I'm going to be busy on Wednesday afternoons."

"Doing what?" I demand.

"Guess."

"I can't," I whine.

"Guess who's been invited to take Ron's advanced ballet class?"

"Peter!" I jump up and clap my hands. I want to throw my arms around his neck. I want to kiss his cheek. Of course I do neither.

Peter has been studying ballet about six months longer than I, but right from the start he had a way of standing out. He's a boy, first of all, and there aren't too many at the academy. But the important thing is that Peter is the most incredible dancer.

I once heard Madame Dukowsky say that dancing is in Peter's blood. And when I watch him in class, I sometimes think he was *born* dancing. He doesn't seem to be struggling like the rest of us. There's something special about Peter, all right, and it's no secret that he is every teacher's favorite. I'm sure he'll be a star one day.

"Don't tell anyone, okay?" he is saying.

"If *I* were invited to take advanced, I'd be shouting it from the rooftops," I answer. "It's a good thing I like you, Peter, or I could easily hate you for being so good."

"You *are* a good dancer," he tells me.

"Not good enough."

We walk up the two dingy flights to the New York Ballet Academy. Piano music filters through long, narrow hallways. It is always extra-crowded here on Saturdays, and while waiting for class to start we clutter the halls, talking in huddles, stretching out across the floor. Some of the kids drink small containers of orange juice and eat yogurt as if it were going out of style.

I climb across a contorted body and peer into one of the dance studios. The door is open a crack.

A floor-to-ceiling mirror spans an entire wall. Opposite, a dozen timid children in first or second grade flounder at the *barre*. Most of them look rigid and unhappy. Their teacher, Corwin, paces up and back, pulling in a stomach, straightening a leg. He doesn't miss a beat as he drones on, ". . . and one, and two . . . heels together, Hilary . . . and three, and four . . . shoulders down, Marilyn . . . and one, and two . . ."

"Psssst." Peter waves to me from the announcement board. "Look at this," he half whispers, "tryouts for the best summer school in the city!"

I read the small printed bulletin.

ATTENTION SENIOR BALLET STUDENTS
Audition for National
Ballet Summer School
March 16
SEE MADAME DUKOWSKY AT DESK
FOR MORE INFORMATION
REMEMBER: SENIOR STUDENTS ONLY!

"This is it, Kate!" Peter is delirious. His dance bag slips off his shoulder to the floor and he absent-mindedly kicks it between his feet. He grabs my shoulders and looks me square in the eye.

I feel my face getting pink and warm.

". . . either now or never," he is saying. But I am concentrating on the blue-green of his eyes. They're like little electric lights, blinking Christmas lights. . . .

"Don't you see?" he sighs.

"See what?"

"Are you listening?" he demands.

"I am. I'm listening." I lie.

"Now, pay attention." His tone of voice is serious. "Here's our big chance! If we take summer classes at the National Ballet School," he says the last three words slowly, and he hangs on every syllable, "we'll really be on our way."

"Sure, Peter," I interrupt. "They're just sitting there waiting for the two of us."

"We'll never know if we don't try," he says.

"I bet *hundreds* of kids will show up for that audition!" I exclaim.

"So what?"

"So what?" I repeat. But even as I say the words, my head is spinning.

I have just auditioned, and the judges remain pinned to their seats. Finally, they begin to whisper among themselves. *The tall blonde*, they buzz, *she is perfect. Don't let her leave the studio. She will start her professional training immediately. An ideal, a dream,* they ogle. *We will sculpt her into the ballerina of the century. . . .*

"Are you there, Kate?" Peter is waving his hand in front of my eyes. "Daydreaming again?" His smile is smug.

"M.Y.O.B." I tell him. "Mind your own business."

"Don't forget," Peter answers, "March the sixteenth."

"Don't forget," I mimic, "March the sixteenth." Then I pat his shoulder and smile. "I'll tell you what," I say quietly, "*you* go to the audition and you can tell me all about it. Meanwhile, I'll go in here." I point to the yellow sign marked "Girls' Dressing Room."

I slip through the door but hear him call out, "I *am* going. But you're coming with me, you'll see!"

If only I were good enough, Peter . . .

The dressing room is noisy and crowded and smells as if someone forgot to open a window. Girls, everywhere girls. Sprawled across narrow wooden benches, they tug at jeans, pull on leotards and tights and sweat shirts and leg warmers. They squeeze in front of the single tiny mirror for last-minute beauty details.

Most of us tie our hair back for class, reinforcing the strays with an elaborate assortment of rubber bands and barrettes, kerchiefs and bobby pins. I love to watch the more daring girls create dark exotic eyes from their plain dull ones. They use fancy looking mascaras and multicolored pencils and they make me feel as if the blusher I bought in Woolworth's were no big deal at all.

I sit in the corner on the cool gray floor to unlace my sneakers. All around me they are talking about the National Ballet School bulletin.

"Madame says the auditions would be a waste of

time for Ballet Two students." Susan Thorndike's
voice has great authority.

"Naturally." That is Lucy Framington. Lucy has
been studying at our school since kindergarten, and
most of us agree she is one of the most obnoxious
people in Manhattan. "Unless you've been on toe
for two years, don't bother showing up."

"Are you going to audition?" Sarah Albright tosses
a chocolate kiss into my lap, then sits on the edge of
the narrow bench in front of me.

*Of course, I am! Everyone knows I'm good enough for
that kind of competition.* That's what I would like to
say, and believe, but instead I answer with a shrug.
"I don't know." I pull a bright yellow T-shirt over
my head and my chest is labeled "Forever Dancing." "What about you?"

Sarah shakes her head. "Not me. I don't have a
prayer."

"We'll never know if we don't try," I tell her,
realizing that Peter said the same thing to me just
five minutes ago.

It's important to stretch out before class, but
today I have dallied too long. Our teacher, Ron, is
already in the studio. He sips steamy coffee and
flirts with the female pianist. Suddenly he looks up.
All chattering stops. And the stretching. Ron puts
out his stub of a cigarette, the final sign that he is
ready. I race to the *barre,* like the others, and squeeze
between Ariane Dukowsky and Peter.

"We begin," Ron announces, unsmiling. "Left hand
on the *barre.* And *plié.*"

Ron Vlostic is a very mysterious and much-talked-about teacher at the academy. It's easy to see why a lot of the girls around here get babyish crushes on him. He is not only glamorous and sexy but exceedingly handsome—movie star caliber. His nose is so straight, cheekbones so high and angular, you would swear someone had chiseled them to perfection. He has olive skin and short black hair and eyes as dark as the Hudson River on a winter's night.

Ron claims he once danced with the Bolshoi Ballet in Moscow, and he is always dropping hints about love affairs with European ballerinas. Some people say he is rich and famous and that he is descended from Russian aristocracy.

"Hips under. Neck lo-o-ong." He places two cold fingers under my chin. They smell of nicotine.

Battement tendu. My eyes are glued to the back of Ariane's head. As usual, Ron stops to praise her flawless extension. Ariane Dukowsky's mother happens to own the academy and Miss Darling Daughter is the most perfect person I've ever seen. Perfect face. A perfect skinny body. Worst of all, Ariane is a perfect dance student.

Frappé. From across the room the voice booms, "Kate! Point that foot until it hurts." I point my foot and it hurts. *"Now* you are working," Ron informs me as if I don't already know it.

Do I ever hate being singled out like that. Sometimes I wish Ron would just leave me alone, but Peter says I should be happy he corrects me. He says Ron wouldn't criticize so much if he didn't think I had potential. But of course, it's easy for Peter to talk.

". . . supporting leg straight, Sarah Albright."

The big hand on the studio clock creeps through our *barre* exercises. Twenty minutes. Twenty-three minutes. I am hot. I am sweaty. I am hungry. Ron walks by and I pray he doesn't see the bent knee or the hip that lifts. I pray he doesn't see the mistakes I don't even know I'm making.

Later I peel off pale pink leg warmers and the yellow T-shirt. We have done our *battements*, *petitis*, and *grands*, on the floor and off. We have done all those exercises that are supposed to strengthen muscles in our feet, our legs, our backs, our fronts. We move out to center floor, which is a lot more fun, but also more difficult.

Away from the *barre* there's a whole new set of things to concentrate on, like the way we move our heads, the *port de bras* (arm position), and *épaulement* (shoulder position). Ron says this is when we begin to bring "an artistic life" to even our most basic ballet exercises.

During this part of class we usually work in three lines across the studio, with Ron choosing the day's stars for the first line, the flunkies for last. Peter and Ariane are always asked to go to the first row. Once in a while I am too, but mostly Ron sends me to the second. I hate not being best, but sometimes it's good to watch the others try out a new movement or position before I have to do it.

It isn't until the last ten or fifteen minutes of class, though, that I remind myself why I want so badly to be a dancer. There I am—jumping, leaping, spinning. (But of course everything has a fancy French name like *assemblé*, *jeté*, and *pirouette*.) Finally, I am *going* somewhere, even if it's only across the floor of a run-down dance studio on the Upper West Side. Springing into *pas de chat*, I catch a glimpse of myself in the mirror and believe, even for a second, that I'm dancing. Dancing!

By the end of our *allegro* combination I am breathing heavily. My face is flushed scarlet, and the perspiration that started as a trickle on my forehead more than an hour ago leaves telltale splotches across my blue leotard as it creeps down, down, down to the sticky soles of my feet.

The official way to end a ballet class is with *révérence* (a bow or curtsy that makes you feel as if you have just performed at the Metropolitan Opera House). Then there's a round of applause for the teacher (by this time you remember where you really are).

We begin to file out of the studio. "Your attention, please," Ron calls to us, then pulls a cigarette, long and skinny, from a flat gold case. The pianist leans across her bench to light it for him. "Students who intend to audition for the National Ballet Summer School, stay a moment," he says.

Nobody moves.

"Shhhhhhhh!"

"Quiet! Ron is going to tell us something."

"Girls and boys." Ron speaks in a low monotone. "As you all know, March sixteenth is only two months away. In the spirit of giving you every advantage for a successful audition, I will be holding supplemental classes on Tuesday and Thursday afternoons at 3:30. Because of their specialized and intensive nature, I'm sorry to report they will be expensive—twice as costly as your regular classes."

"I'll pay anything!" shrieks Lucy Framington.

"But I have flute on Thursdays," somebody whines.

Ron inhales deeply. "A serious dancer will find a way to be here." He turns on his heel and leaves the studio.

We are dismissed.

"I wonder if my grandmother will go along with the extra classes," I say to Peter en route to our separate dressing rooms.

"I thought you didn't want to audition." He is smug.

"I never said anything of the sort, Peter Robinson. And besides," I add smoothly, "a few extra classes may be just what it takes to push me over the edge—and on to stardom."

Peter laughs and gives my shoulder a friendly nudge. "See you in a few minutes."

4

The minute my key is in the door I can tell something funny is going on. First I hear muffled voices in the kitchen. Then Pinky leaps out of the bathroom.

"You're here!" she cries and practically knocks me down. Hair dripping, a soggy towel around her neck, she takes my arm and leads me toward our bedroom.

"Let go," I hiss as she carefully closes the door behind us. I collapse into the old wooden rocker, kick off drab olive sneakers. "Do you need a podium or can you just tell me what's going on? I need a hot bath, Pinky," I say impatiently. "What's up?"

She flips her head, spraying me with tiny water pellets. "It's Mr. Schumacher!" she exclaims.

I swear, my sister is the most exasperating person. She says things out of the blue, like "It's Mr.

Schumacher!" as if I'm supposed to know right away what she means.

"What are you talking about?" I close my eyes and lean back in the chair.

"They've been in the kitchen with the door closed—for two hours," she says breathlessly.

"Who?"

"Nana and Mr. Schumacher, that's who!" she blurts out.

"Why is that such a big deal?" I rock back and forth, back and forth, feeling very relaxed. "They always sit around talking about the old days," I remind her.

"But I heard him crying!" she wails.

"Pinky." I sit up straight, shake a warning finger. "You shouldn't spy on an old man like that."

"I was not spying," she says. "You couldn't help hearing him." Here come the wide eyes and trembly lip. I hand her a tissue because the tears come next.

"I guess he's real sad," I suggest, "with Mrs. Schumacher being dead and all."

"Except for Whiskers, he's all alone." My sister crumples the yellow tissue into a ball, aims for the wastebasket.

"Whiskers is a nice dog, Pinky, but probably he isn't much company for a man like Mr. Schumacher."

Suddenly the front door shuts and we listen for Nana's steady footsteps in the foyer, the living room, the narrow hall that leads to our bedroom.

"Pinky? Kate?" She knocks softly, then opens the bedroom door.

"Hi."

My grandmother looks the way she always does after cleaning the apartment all day. Her hair is defluffed and a mess, her skin is pale, and the bright blue eyes look unmistakably overcast. Sitting on the edge of Pinky's bed, she says, "We must talk."

"What's wrong with Mr. Schumacher?" Pinky asks.

"Blow your nose." Nana pulls a wrinkled tissue from her apron pocket. I lean forward in my chair to stop the rocking.

"You both know that Mr. Schumacher is a very fine lawyer," Nana begins. "Years ago he worked his way through law school, then made his way up the letterhead in that big shot Wall Street firm of his."

"We already know that," says Pinky impatiently.

"All of a sudden," Nana continues, "they come up with a new rule down there that says a person has to retire at seventy."

"I think that's very nice," Pinky declares. "Now he can move to Florida, like all the old people do."

"You may find this hard to believe," says Nana, "but seventy is not old! It's only when everyone starts telling a person how old he is that he begins to feel that way."

"Can he get another job?" I ask.

Nana shakes her head. "Mr. Schumacher has made the rounds. They all tell him the same thing. 'Take a rest, Max. You've earned it . . . go on a trip,' they say." Nana stands abruptly. "Forty-five

years he devotes his life to the law and now they tell
the man to take a rest. It's disgusting."

"What will he do?" Pinky is sitting cross-legged
on the floor beneath the window. Her expression
has become so intense that little crinkles line her
forehead.

"For starters," Nana clears her throat, "he would
like to spend more time here, with us."

"Great," I say.

But there is something about the way Nana pulls
at her fingers that makes me wonder what it is she's
trying to say. *More time here, with us?* Mr. Schumacher is not exactly a stranger around here. We're
always inviting him to dinner. And what about all
those nights when he appears with a pot of delicious-
smelling coffee? He and Nana manage to stay up,
talking away, long after I've gone to bed.

". . . Whiskers, too?" Pinky is asking.

"Yes. He will come with Whiskers," Nana says
slowly. "They will both come."

"Nana," I say, more than a little curious now,
"just how much time does Mr. Schumacher want to
spend here?"

"Well," she hesitates, "a lot."

"You make it sound as if he wants to move in." I
am only half kidding.

"He is very lonely," Nana answers.

"A dog! We'll have a dog!" Pinky is on her feet,
turning little circles in front of me.

"Cut that out!" I yell.

"He hates being alone in the apartment now that

dear Mrs. Schumacher is gone. And with this retirement business it means spending long, dreary days there," Nana tells us. "He says he simply can't do it. Too many memories."

"But why us?" I ask. "What about his own children?"

"Kate," she says, "you know that his sons live in California. Mr. Schumacher's home is here in New York."

"But *live* here?" My voice is a squeak. Nana's eyes tell me I am disappointing her, but somehow I can't help myself.

"It's a period of adjustment for him," she is saying. "He will pay rent, naturally. He insists on that, and we can certainly use the money."

"I don't understand," I say defiantly. "He pays rent upstairs in 14A."

"Whiskers! He'll live here too!" cries Pinky and I fight the urge to shove her in the closet.

"Calm down, Pinky," says Nana. I search that soft, familiar face for a clue, some sign that she doesn't really mean to do this.

"Max Schumacher is a proud man, but now he feels useless," she continues. "Everyone needs a reason to get up in the morning. Kate, you have school, and of course your ballet, and your friends," she points out. "Frankly, you and Pinky are *my* reason."

"We are?" I am staring out the window. Somewhere among the aluminum garbage cans in the alley a cat is whining. Poor fellow, he must be hungry and cold.

I remember how Grampa loved the alley cats. A special breed of survivors, he called them. The thought of Grampa triggers something in my head, like a private picture show. In a flash I see three distinct scenes: Pinky, Grampa, and me sledding in Riverside Park; Grampa and me presenting Nana with hot bagels and fresh cream cheese after one of our chatty Sunday morning walks; Grampa lugging the heavy picnic basket all the way to our favorite shady spot in Central Park. Since Nana refused to share her lunch with the "ants and nature," it was just Grampa, Pinky, and me on those sunny afternoons.

". . . to tell the truth," Nana is saying, "it was *my* suggestion that Mr. Schumacher stay here. For a while, anyway."

"You invited him?" I don't mean to sound so nasty, but the words are already past my lips.

She turns to me with those disappointed eyes of hers. "We don't desert our friends when they need us, Kate. You mustn't forget we've known the Schumachers for many years."

"How many?" asks Pinky.

Then Nana smiles for the first time this afternoon. "I never stopped to count," she says, "but probably close to forty."

Pinky whistles. I press my nose, hard, against the cold pane. It's dark out now, and in the blackness of the window I follow Nana's movements as she smooths the bedspread, fluffs a pillow.

"Your Grampa used to say that things have a way of working out for the best." Nana raises her eyebrows and shrugs. "We'll have to wait and see."

"Nana?"

"Yes, Kate."

"Do you mean he'll be here for always, like another Grampa?" I ask.

Her sigh is long and soft, like the air escaping from a bicycle tire. She sits on the old rocker, then pulls me to her. I rest my head on her lap, the way I did when I was little.

"My great sadness is that you girls learned much, much too early that nothing is for always." But then her voice lifts, and I sense that she is smiling. "And besides, if it doesn't work out with Mr. Schumacher, where's the great tragedy? We'll just send him packing if he doesn't watch his step!"

I hug her waist. "Nana?"

"Yes, Kate."

"Where will he sleep?"

She rubs my head. "Why, he'll sleep in the den, of course."

That's supposed to be my room, I want to remind her. But she is talking on. "There's the foldaway bed and a bookshelf, and we'll need to make some room in that closet . . ."

"Can Whiskers sleep in our room?" Pinky must be feeling neglected because she has started doing a series of somersaults in the skinny aisle between our beds.

"Whiskers may not sleep in your room," Nana tells her. "Now how about some dinner around here — I'm starved."

"Me too."

"Kate, you soak away those tight muscles in a warm tub, and we'll be ready to eat in fifteen minutes."

"Nana?" Now I am bold. "What would Grampa say?"

Her mouth twists into a funny little smile. "I think he would be pleased."

"I wish he was here," says Pinky.

Nana nods. "So do I," she whispers, "so do I."

5

Pinky made the sign: "Mr. Schumacher's Place."

"Very classy," I tell her, as she tapes it slightly off center to the den door.

It's funny, the way some things happen so fast. One minute Nana comes up with this brainstorm and the next thing I know it's moving day. In no time at all Mr. Schumacher managed to sublet his apartment to a young lawyer named Rodney Falloway. Then he packed up—one trunk, one medium-sized suitcase, and four cartons of books.

Last week we cleared out the den in three stages. First we dragged Nana's antiquated sewing machine to her bedroom in order to make a space for the single piece of furniture Mr. Schumacher is moving from 14A. It's a beautiful oak writing table. He told me he brought it all the way from the old country half a century ago, and it had once been his father's.

Next we emptied bookshelves because Nana in-sisted Mr. Schumacher would feel more at home with his own books.

"Don't you think it's time, Kate, to give away some of these?" She was standing on the creaky stepladder, a dustrag in one hand and two tall pic-ture books in the other.

"No, not yet," I insisted, carefully turning the well-worn pages of my *Madeline*. After all these years the little girls were still in their straight lines. . . .

But the best part of the conversion of the den to Mr. Schumacher's Place was that cold Sunday after-noon when Nana, Pinky, and I attempted to make room for his things in the overstuffed walk-in closet. What treasures we found! We sifted through rows of dresses, all Nana's, and some dating as far back as her courtship with Grampa. Multicolored boxes were piled to the ceiling. There were shoeboxes and hatboxes, boxes labeled "Hair ribbons" and others labeled "Lingerie." It's hard to believe my grand-mother ever spent so much time, and money, on herself.

"Here! I wore this to your Great-Aunt Mildred's wedding." Nana was holding up a raspberry-colored smock of a dress. "I was slightly pregnant," she added.

"I can't imagine you pregnant."

"I wasn't born this old, Kate."

"Look at me!" Pinky had zipped herself into a skinny yellow dress. It hugged her ankles and dragged on the floor, but she managed to step up on the sofa bed so we could properly admire her.

"When your Grampa graduated from City College, his parents made a splash of a party. I think half the Bronx showed up!" Nana laughed. "I wore this slinky yellow number, believe it or not."

"I hope you looked better in that dress than Pinky does." I was busy trying on a big-brimmed straw hat, and we all burst out laughing when it slipped over my ears to rest on the bridge of my nose.

"You'll see," Nana told us periodically, "if you hold on to your clothes long enough, they all come back in style."

And once I caught her crying quietly into Grampa's favorite plaid muffler. "It's my whole life," she murmured, "staring me in the face."

In the end we made very little room for Mr. Schumacher's things. Having decided there was nothing Nana could part with, we rehung the dresses, returned pointy-toed shoes to their boxes, and closed the closet door with a mind to keep the past tucked neatly away. "That way," Nana told us, "it's always there when you need it."

It is late Thursday afternoon and I am stuck, sardine-style, on the Seventh Avenue subway. I'm in a big hurry because this was Mr. Schumacher's Moving-in Day, and I'm dying to see what's going on. Pinky and I thought we should stay home from school for the big event, but of course, my grandmother had other ideas. Anyway, Ron's supplemental class was at 3:30 and that's one thing I won't give up—not for Mr. Schumacher or anybody.

The academy is really buzzing these days. It's funny because even though most of us deny wanting to audition for the National Ballet School, everyone seems to be showing up on Tuesday and Thursday afternoons. Everyone but me. I have pleaded and begged, but Nana insists that one class, in addition to Saturday, is plenty.

"You don't understand," I griped, "I'll *never* be a star if you don't let me go both days."

"If God wants you to be a star, you'll make it with or without the extra class," she told me. "And besides, we just can't afford it."

"Peter says all the serious dancers—the good ones—are there both days," I persisted.

It was like talking to the wall.

Ballet has suddenly become a deadly serious business. There is no more gabbing and fooling around in the dressing room before a class. Instead, we all head straight to the studio to warm up. Nobody smiles. Nobody makes a face behind our teacher's back. Nobody complains that the *barre* is too difficult or too long. And Ron is even more uptight and unfriendly than usual, often hinting at the wonderful publicity our school would get if any of us made the National Ballet School.

More than ever before, my body is challenged. My brain is challenged. The truth is I am a little bit relieved that Nana is sticking to her Thursday/Saturday rule. Every week I find muscles I'm sure weren't there before, new aches to soothe in a hot tub and for Nana to rub away. It would all be worth it if only the studio mirrors were my friend. But now, when I can't afford to be less than perfect, they mock my lack of skill and keep me from looking just right.

Having fought my way out of the smoldering subway, I execute three *grands jetés* in the semidarkness of 109th Street. I suppose Peter is right about one thing. If we make NBS, we are on our way to the top. Imagine, *me* taking class five, maybe six days a week! Of course, I would go to the Professional Children's School instead of P.S. 62. Later on, Peter and I would be *pas de deux* partners. I can see the headlines now: *Bravo, Kate! Bravo, Peter! This evening New Yorkers were treated to the exquisite and sensitive premiere performance of Miss Kate Newman and Mr. Peter Robinson in* Swan Lake. *Keep your eye on these two because they are going places.* . . .

At the front door of the apartment I am greeted by an avalanche—an avalanche named Whiskers. He bounces off the floor, then lands on his hind legs, again and again. Crazy dog.

"Down, boy. Down." I twist out of his way. "Anybody home?" I call out as I follow the crazy one to the kitchen.

As usual, Nana is flying between the stove and refrigerator. Pinky is folding paper napkins into meticulous, though uneven rectangles. And Mr. Schumacher, looking strangely a part of things, is busy shredding potatoes at the kitchen table. Shredding potatoes in Nana's kitchen?

I clear my throat. "Hi."

Three sets of eyes fall on me.

"Kate. We didn't hear you come in." Nana kisses my forehead, then gently pivots me toward Mr. Schumacher. Very subtle, my grandmother.

"Good evening, Mr. Schumacher."

"Hello, Kate." He smiles, a little shyly, I notice, then turns back to his potatoes and his shredding.

"How was your day?" Nana asks me.

"Okay. I got eighty-five on the algebra quiz."

"Good!" she exclaims. "It looks like Peter is a terrific coach after all. And how did the ballet go this afternoon?"

"Okay." I shrug, thinking about the *six* times Ron picked on me. "So what's for supper?" I ask no one in particular.

"Pot roast and Mr. Schumacher's special potatoes," Pinky answers. "It's a secret recipe, right, Mr. Schumacher?"

"Well," he winks, "I'm willing to share the secret." He points to the glass bowl on the kitchen table. "This is called *rosti*," he says. "First grate your potatoes, like I'm doing now. Next chop an onion, season with salt and pepper, and sauté the whole thing until it's nice and brown."

"Sounds good," I say.

"Sounds pretty fattening for ballerinas on diets," Pinky warns in her sweetest tone of voice.

Ten minutes later I don't believe my own eyes. Mr. Schumacher is stationed at the stove, stirring up his *rosti*. Nana has the weirdest expression on her face, as if she's expecting him to goof up, but she is smiling and making silly jokes about being pushed out of her own kitchen. Watching her, I am beginning to feel the tiniest bit in the way.

"Come, girls!" She claps her hands a little too loud. "Supper is ready. Comb your hair, Kate. Pinky, have you put out the water pitcher?"

We push the round table away from the wall to make room for Mr. Schumacher. I don't think he means to, but he sits right down in Grampa's chair, under the house phone that doesn't work. Funny, he never sat there before, all those times he came for dinner. Nana always did. I wonder if she notices.

If she does, my grandmother certainly doesn't let on. Instead, she smiles warmly and raises her water glass in a toast. "Welcome, Mr. Schumacher. Welcome to our home."

"That is lovely, Mrs. Stein," he practically whispers, "very lovely indeed."

Leave it to Nana to make a person feel good.

We are incredibly formal tonight and it isn't even the *Shabbas*. Nana, serving from her place at the table, is very grand about putting a proper amount of pot roast and *rosti* on our plates. There are fresh string beans in a red bowl and a dish of applesauce for each of us.

By the time we stop passing things around, my arms are tired, and so is my mouth, from smiling. I am convinced we look like one of those TV families, the kind that has fantastic dinner conversations every single night.

But there happens to be one big difference. *We*

aren't talking. I take a long drink of water. Through the bottom of the glass I am able to look from Nana to Mr. Schumacher to Pinky. Why doesn't one of them say something? Doesn't this deadly silence bother anyone but me? What's the problem here . . .?

"Yikes!" I jump up and my chair falls backward with a clatter. "Something is crawling up my leg!"

Of all things, Mr. Schumacher begins to laugh. Then Nana and Pinky. I am outraged—until Pinky pulls herself together and points her index finger in my direction. Whiskers has poked his head from beneath the table. A piece of potato is stuck to his nose. His head is cocked and I swear that nutty dog is smiling at me. I cross my eyes and stick out my tongue. He barks once and I know we are friends.

"So you're the thumper!" I laugh at the stubby tail that drums against the vinyl floor. "You nearly scared me to death, Whiskers." I pat his head between stick-up Airedale ears, drop a piece of potato into his mouth. "Try *eating* it this time," I suggest.

"He likes your cooking, Mr. Schumacher," says Pinky.

"So do I," declares Nana. "This is fine *rosti*, Max Schumacher. I'm terribly impressed."

Tonight we are four—washing, drying, and putting dishes away. Every couple of minutes Nana suggests that one or another of us leave because there's simply no room. But we all stay. Politely bumping into each other. Mr. Schumacher keeps asking where this belongs, or that, and he insists on climbing Nana's stepladder so he can reach the highest cabinets.

When the last plate is stacked, the last pot hidden from sight, Nana unties her apron and pushes the hair off her forehead with the back of her hand.

"Kate," she says, "why don't you and Pinky take Whiskers for a short walk?"

"Pinky doesn't have to come," I answer. "I'd rather go alone." What I really want is to practice my *grands jetés en tournant* up and down 109th Street. It seemed as if I were the only one who couldn't get it right in class today, and if Ron corrected me one more time, I knew I'd leave the studio in tears.

"I am coming," Pinky announces, winning again.

Privacy certainly has a way of passing me by. Two minutes later I am zipping up my ski parka when Mr. Schumacher comes into the front foyer in his big brown duffle coat. Whiskers, dragging the leather leash in his mouth, is running circles around him. I feel like sighing loudly, but I don't. What's the use?

"Mr. Schumacher is coming, too," Pinky informs me as she slips her hand into his. *Baby.* "He's going to show us the ropes with Whiskers."

"And," says Mr. Schumacher, hooking the leash onto Whiskers's collar, "I love the night air."

"Maybe I should stay in and do my French homework." As soon as the words are out of my mouth, I know I shouldn't have said them. I know because I hear the way it sounds, and because of the hurt look on Mr. Schumacher's face.

"You know something?" he says quietly. "I'm awfully tired from the move, and I haven't even read the *Times* yet. Why don't you girls go ahead—I'm sure you can handle old Whiskers."

Cripes, I've really done it this time. Nana will kill me. "No," I say, "gosh, of course you'll go. I mean, we'll all go, Mr. Schumacher. Here," I stammer, "here's my coat, and yours too . . ."

A few minutes later we are huddled against the wind. Whiskers, obviously master of his walks, leads Pinky on his leash. Except for the occasional yellow streetlamp that casts gloomy shadows on the sidewalk, Riverside Drive is pitch-black.

"Shouldn't we walk on Broadway?" Pinky asked as we turned right toward the Drive.

"Too many people on Broadway," Mr. Schumacher answered. "Whiskers prefers the peace and quiet."

"It's beautiful out here tonight." I am trying hard to prove I'm not such a bad person. "Reminds me of a Hitchcock movie, only I'm not scared. By the way, have you heard my grandmother absolutely forbids us to walk on the Drive at night?"

I look up at Mr. Schumacher with what I hope is a friendly twinkle in my eye. But he is gazing ahead, looking very tall and skinny, even in the thick coat. His dark knitted sailor's cap is pulled over his ears, completely hiding the curly gray hair. How different from Grampa, who had hardly any hair at all! I remember how he went to the barber anyway, every single week, to keep it just right. . . .

"Are you trying to say that an old man like me

has to abide by your grandmother's rules!" The
corners of Mr. Schumacher's mouth turn up, ever
so slightly. Thank goodness.

"You better believe it," I smile. "She's a tough
lady."

Pinky and Whiskers are skipping ahead. Every
few yards my sister turns to us and waves happily.

"Pinky sure likes that dog," Mr. Schumacher
remarks.

"There's going to be a battle to keep him in our
room tonight. Wait and see." In spite of the cold
night air, I am warming up; my body is beginning
to relax. It isn't that I don't like Mr. Schumacher. I
would hate for him to think that. But he must
understand he just isn't one of us. . . .

"Your classes in ballet," he is saying, "are you
content with your progress?"

I shrug. "I guess so." It's funny that he would
talk about my dancing. Progress? Is that what you
call the mess I've been making in every single class
lately? Anyway, who stops to think about it? It's
work, Mr. Schumacher, plain hard work.

"Then you are anxious to continue?"

Well, I guess Mr. Schumacher doesn't understand who it is he's talking to! Kate B. Newman is
going places. Why, she's going to be a famous ballerina, lovely and unique. . . . "Yes." I answer, very
solemn. "I may even go on to the National Ballet
School this summer."

Cripes! For the second time tonight, I've blurted
out something I didn't mean to say. For goodness

sake, I can't be blabbing all my private thoughts to Mr. Schumacher. I haven't even decided if I'm going to audition on March 16.

"That's wonderful!" he exclaims. "I'm so happy for you, Kate." Mr. Schumacher and I stand facing each other under a yellow streetlamp.

"Well," I hesitate, "I need to have an audition first. It isn't as if you can just *go* to the National Ballet School." I don't want Mr. Schumacher getting any ideas about what a star I am before I really am one. Nana will kill me for bragging.

"If you want something badly enough," he says slowly, "I think you are the kind of girl who will get it, Kate."

I look down at my toes, wondering if that isn't the nicest thing anyone has ever said to me. I want to say thank you, but somehow the words won't come.

6

"I'm home!" I announce.

"In here," Mr. Schumacher calls from the kitchen. I find him peering into the oven. Nana's yellow checkered apron is tied around his waist.

"What smells so good?" I ask. "Where's my grandmother? Is Pinky home yet?"

Mr. Schumacher twists his head to look at me. "Cookies. At the supermarket. Yes."

"I beg your pardon?"

He gently closes the oven door. "I am answering your questions. In order: I am baking cookies. Mrs. Stein is shopping at the A&P. And Pinky is either working on her movie star scrapbook or doing homework. In either case," he winks, "she doesn't seem to be practicing piano."

I am balancing on one foot, yanking the boot from the other. "Need help?" Mr. Schumacher asks.

I fall backward onto one of the wrought-iron ice cream chairs. "What kind of cookies?" I ask. The boot is off, finally.

"Chocolate chip. Do you like them?"

"You better believe it!"

"I've been told," he says, sitting in the chair across the table from me, "that my cookies rate with the best in town."

"No kidding." My toes are numb from the cold and I start kneading them with ten half-frozen fingers.

Mr. Schumacher holds Nana's plastic spatula in the air. His eyes are fixed on the face of an expensive-looking watch. "Four minutes left for this batch," he says.

"Good."

"You know," he continues, without looking up, "timing is everything, Kate. In cooking and in life."

"No kidding," I say again, absently.

"Like with Mrs. Schumacher and myself. Had I met her just one month later, I would have been married to another girl! You see," he goes on, "my parents, may they rest in peace, had already arranged for my marriage."

"What do you mean?" I ask, wondering when the aches in my toes will go away. "How did they arrange it?"

"In our little village back in the old country there was a regular matchmaker—Zytl. She decided that the baker's daughter and the tailor's son were a perfect match. Zap! A little money exchanged, and the whole thing is arranged."

"I thought things like that only happened in the movies," I tell him. "Did you like the baker's daughter?"

Mr. Schumacher's soft gray eyes are dancing now. They dart back and forth from his watch to my face. "It just so happens the baker's daughter was the homeliest girl in the village."

"Oh, no!" I laugh. "How could they expect you to marry her?"

"What could a young boy do?" he shrugs. "An arrangement is an arrangement."

"Then how did you meet Mrs. Schumacher?" I ask.

"Ah! That was the miracle, and every day I thank God for bringing her to me. You see, Kate, Mrs. Schumacher didn't live in the village. She was visiting her cousins—very wealthy and properly religious people.

"It is a beautiful October morning," he continues. "I am rushing through the village center when suddenly I stop dead in my tracks. I am stone, unable to move. A beautiful dark-eyed stranger is prancing along the dirt road. She swings a bucket, and I am in love."

Wow! I can see it now—a young and handsome Max Schumacher stuck with the ugliest girl in town, and suddenly he falls in love. Love at first sight, just like in the movies . . .

"She was a jewel," Mr. Schumacher reminisces. The funny thing is I don't remember Mrs. Schumacher's being any great beauty, but they say beauty is in the eye of the beholder—or something like that.

"Then what happened?" I ask, noticing that Mr. Schumacher's quiet smile looks past me. His eyes have that faraway look that Nana gets when she lights the Sabbath candles.

"Luckily," he answers, "I found my legs again and ran after her. But when I caught up, I was so nervous I couldn't say a word. Imagine how foolish I felt. She smiled at my eyes, though, before skipping off. I was smitten," he concludes.

"What about the other girl—the ugly one?" I ask.

"I'll get to that," he tells me. "So, there I was, three weeks from my wedding to the baker's daughter and irrationally in love with a girl whose name I didn't know."

"Poor Mr. Schumacher . . ."

"Now I will tell you about the miracle," he announces with much ado. "The Ashers—those were the cousins I told you about—were giving a formal dinner."

"And you were invited!" I guess excitedly.

"I certainly was not invited. Tailors' sons did not go to parties of people like the Ashers. But," and now he points his finger in the air, "a certain tailor's son did deliver Mr. Asher's new slacks."

"Fantastic!"

"With Mr. Solomon Asher's new gray trousers tucked under my arm, I knock on that eminent door. Who should pull it open but the dark-eyed stranger. A miracle."

I lean across the table. "Did you ask her for a date?"

"No dates, Kate. You forget I was engaged to be married," he answers. "Besides, who had money for dates?"

"Tell me, Mr. Schumacher. Tell me how you and Mrs. Schumacher finally got together."

"Looking back, I don't know where I got the nerve, but I proposed to her the very next day." Mr. Schumacher shakes his head as if he still can't believe it.

I clap my hands together and shriek, "Wow!"

Now Mr. Schumacher's eyes are half-closed. "She said yes," he practically whispers, "and that was that."

I sigh happily, then remember one unfinished part of this beautiful and romantic story. "The baker's daughter, Mr. Schumacher. Whatever happened to the baker's daughter?"

"Well," he begins, but suddenly he jumps up, crying, "The cookies! The cookies!"

In the rush to the oven, I trip on Mr. Schumacher's heel. *"Kaput!"* I start laughing so hard that I fall doubled over to my knees. A smoking mess assaults my eyes and nose. Mr. Schumacher is removing the charred black crisps from the oven. I swear they're stuck to Nana's aluminum cookie sheet forever. *"Kaput,* like the baker's daughter," I manage to sputter before dropping to my elbows in uncontrolled hysteria.

Before I know what's happening, Mr. Schumacher

is sitting on the floor beside me, holding his knees to his chest and laughing loudly. We pinch our noses against the nauseating smell of burning chocolate.

Eventually I can raise my head. Through watery eyes I see Pinky and Nana standing over us, four hands on two sets of hips.

"What's the big joke?" Pinky asks suspiciously.

Mr. Schumacher and I never get a chance to answer. We're too busy rolling on the floor like a couple of hyenas.

7

Early Saturday morning I pad out to the kitchen for some hot chocolate. I'm surprised to find Mr. Schumacher sitting at the table. His face is long and his shoulders sag.

"Good morning, Kate," he mumbles, staring into space.

"Are you okay?" I yawn loudly and adjust the buttons of my pajama top. Stretching both hands way over my head, I flop over to rest my palms on the floor.

"Ach," he says impatiently, "I had one of those nights—too little sleep, too much thinking. It isn't good, to think so hard."

"I'll make cocoa," I suggest cheerfully.

"Good idea." He pats Whiskers's back and between his ears. "We're getting lazy, old fellow. Retirement is for the birds."

I set two steamy mugs of cocoa on the table. "Try some whipped cream, Mr. Schumacher. It's good for you."

"You're a sweet girl," he smiles. "I must stop talking about myself."

"But I love it when you talk about yourself." I hand him the can of whipped cream. "Your life was . . . is . . . so interesting compared to ours."

"You're a young girl, Kate. Your whole life is ahead of you. Mine is over. Anyway," he says before I can protest, "you make delicious cocoa."

"Thank you." I squirt two huge globs of whipped cream into my cup. "One of these days I'm going to start drinking coffee. But not yet. Only when I'm fatter."

"Are you planning to fatten up?" Mr. Schumacher's eyes are pastel gray this morning. He is wearing a plaid flannel shirt and preppy-looking corduroy slacks. I wish I had the nerve to tell him I think he looks very nice and young.

"Never," I say emphatically. "The problem is I like to eat."

"And why not?" he asks logically.

"Because I'm going to be a dancer. Did you ever see a fat ballerina?" I start chipping tiny bits of unmelted cocoa powder from the edge of my cup. "Do you think I'm getting a little heavy, Mr. Schumacher?"

"To be honest," he hesitates, "I think you are a little on the skinny side."

"Whew." I lean my head all the way back to

catch the last chocolate drops. "Anyway, I wish I were taller."

"Of course."

I push my chair away from the table. "I'll make more cocoa," I say lightly, "to celebrate the fact that I'm such a string bean."

Waiting for the water to boil, I pull aside the window curtain. "Mr. Schumacher!" I shout. "It's snowing!"

He comes to the window and for several minutes we stand side by side, watching big white puffs of snow sail down, down, down. They land gracefully, on fire escapes, garbage cans, window ledges. "It's sticking," I whisper, not wanting to lose the magic of the moment. "Maybe we'll get lucky and school will be closed for a couple of weeks. But," I add, "not ballet school."

"When I was a boy in Europe, you can be sure the school didn't close down for a little snow," Mr. Schumacher says sternly. "We would have been on holiday from October to May."

"I think snowstorms are kind of romantic, don't you?" I answer.

"Good morning." Nana is standing in the doorway and I don't believe my own eyes. She is wearing the Mother's Day robe instead of the ugly gray housedress. I can't imagine what the occasion is. I'm sure it isn't a birthday or Christmas. It isn't even the Jewish New Year or Thanksgiving.

"You're pretty," I whisper, hooking my arm through hers. I gently guide Nana to her chair, then bow formally from the waist. "Today *nous celebrons,* we celebrate, skinny people," I say solemnly. "On behalf of Mr. Max Schumacher, to my left, and Miss Pinky Newman, asleep in her warm bed, and me, Kate Newman—the most slender ballerina of all time—I extend hearty greetings!"

Nana laughs, then starts to get up. I shake a warning finger. *"Madame,* this morning your loving granddaughter, *la jeune fille,* will serve you."

I return to the table with a cup of instant coffee for Nana and the box of cocoa for Mr. Schumacher and me. It's funny the way they both stop talking, and sit up a little straighter, the minute I sit down.

"How come you're all dressed up, Nana?"

"I am not dressed up, Kate."

"Okay. Whatever you say." I scoop two heaping teaspoons of cocoa powder into the blue mug.

"Did you sleep well, Mrs. Stein?" That's Mr. Schumacher. I'll never figure out why he and Nana insist on calling each other by their last names. After all, they've been friends for a hundred years. Imagine if I started calling Peter Mr. Robinson!

"Thank you," she answers. "I am well rested." So formal! Now I happen to know that my grandmother is one of those people who never seems to sleep. I guess she goes to bed sometime or other, but I'll never figure out when. I remember when I was a little kid, I used to get up a lot in the middle of the night. I'd always find her in the kitchen, reading at the table, or baking. And no matter what time it was, she was wide awake and glad to see me. Me with my nasty dreams and stomachaches.

"Yes. You look quite refreshed this morning." Mr. Schumacher is looking straight at my grandmother. "Your robe, it is very . . . umm . . . becoming." Meanwhile, Nana is studying her coffee cup, and if I didn't know better, I would swear she is blushing.

This is a ridiculous conversation. It's rude, the way they're ignoring me altogether. I have this sick feeling they don't even know I'm in the room.

By the time I leave for dance class the forecast is for heavy snow, continuing through the night and all day Sunday. Nana is griping about my going all the way down to Eighty-sixth Street in the "blizzard,"and Mr. Schumacher practically insists on taking me to the school himself. I'm thoroughly annoyed with the two of them but wangle my way out of the apartment by promising to ring twice the minute I get there.

Downstairs I jump off the bottom step and watch my feet disappear in the morning snow, already three or four inches deep. I look up and down the block. No footsteps. No people. It is safe to tilt the tip of my nose to the sky and let cold fluffs of snow melt on my tongue.

The wind blows snow in my face, and maneuvering to the subway is not nearly as easy as I thought it would be. I am tempted to turn back but can't afford to miss class, not with that audition coming up.

Broadway is really eerie this morning, like a ghost town I once saw in a John Wayne western. The city just doesn't feel right, and it's no wonder. There are no yellow taxis darting through traffic, no city buses grunting and slugging along, no sanitation trucks banging their noisy way down the streets. But the weirdest thing of all is there isn't a soul in sight. In a word, it is too quiet.

The subway takes forever and I am freezing. I pace, up and back, up and back, eyes fastened to the big rusting clock that hangs over the tracks.

"Are the trains running?" I call out to the token seller on the other side of the turnstile. No answer. "Hey, mister," I persist, "are the trains running?"

"Yeah, girlie. It'll come."

You're quite a creep, I would like to tell him, but of course I don't. Besides, the train does rumble into the station, finally, and I take a seat in the nearly empty car.

"Kate!" I jump at the sound of my name. The train screeches out of the station and Peter teeters over to sit next to me. His cheeks are bright from the cold and the tip of his nose is wet. He wipes a green parka sleeve across his face, pulls off the knitted ski band, and shakes his head. In a flash I consider the pros and cons of telling him. The truth. *Peter,* I would say, *darling Peter, I love you.* And he would look into my eyes, and my heart, the way they do in the movies. . . .

". . . he hit the roof," Peter is saying.

"What?" I shout over the din of the train.

"My father hit the roof when I told him about the National Ballet School Audition," he shouts back. "He sat me down in his leather-bound study and announced that no son of his is going to be a dancer."

"That's horrible!" I exclaim. "How could he say such a thing?"

Peter shrugs unhappily. "To show me what a liberal parent he is, he said he won't *forbid* all the extra classes, but he will be 'exceedingly disappointed' in me if I do go on to the National Ballet School."

"Maybe he just doesn't understand how much dancing means to you," I suggest. "Probably he doesn't know how *good* you are."

"He understands," Peter sulks.

"What about your mother, what does she think?"

"You know my mother. To keep peace, she'll go along with whatever he says," Peter answers.

Poor Peter. A bully for a father, a wishy-washy mother. If only they could see him in class, hear the instructors' praise. If only they could watch the rest of us secretly try to copy everything he does. Then they would have to be more supportive.

It's no wonder Peter likes our house so much. Nana would never say such a disgusting thing to him. In fact, she's the one who insists the world needs more boy dancers. Also, she has a way of getting Peter to talk about his dancing. But he's so modest, even with her.

"My source tells me you've been asked to join Ron's advanced class," Nana said to him just last week.

"Your *source* talks too much," Peter blushed, then gave me a dirty look.

"But we are proud of you!" Nana retaliated.

"Thank you."

"You take yourself too seriously," Nana told him.

"I don't."

"I notice," Nana continued, "that you and Kate have been neglecting your friends, replacing them with extra ballet classes."

"We've got to be prepared for that audition," Peter answered.

"Peter," she scolded. "I know ballet is the most important thing in the world to you, but you're all of fourteen, a child. You must get out and have some fun."

"I do have fun," he insisted. "I do."

But Nana shook her head knowingly. "I'm crazy about you, Peter Robinson, and I think I understand you. But you must remember one thing—" she smiled, "you can't fool Jessie Stein."

It turns out there are only three of us in class this stormy afternoon—Peter, me, and, unfortunately, Ariane Dukowsky. Ron shows up a half hour late and he is fuming about the disgraceful way our city falls apart every time it snows. He charges into the studio, arms flailing, an angry cigarette dangling from puffy lips. He flings his red beret toward the empty piano bench, then shakes his head with great flair, so each hair may fall into its proper layered place.

A long purple scarf is wound several times around his neck, and he is wearing a gorgeous furry coat I haven't seen before. He lets the coat slide to the floor and slowly unwinds the scarf. "We begin."

I clutch the *barre*. With one hand planted solidly on his hip and the other rubbing his head, Ron stands a foot to the front and side of me. He folds his cold fingers around mine. "There! *This* is the position of the arm." Gently he pulls my right arm to its perfect position. I'll never get it right. Why, I wonder, why do I torture myself by coming to class? I try to catch Peter's eye in the mirror. I try not to think. Ron says I *think* too much. He says I must relax.

Finally, he moves away and I can breathe again. By tilting my head ever so slightly, I'm able to watch him examine his own torso in the wide mirrors. How vain can a person be? I'll never behave like that, no matter how perfect my body looks. . . .

"Kate Newman!" he calls to me in the mirror. "That hip must remain stationary. The leg will move as a unit from the hip." I might as well be a first-year ballet student, the way he's treating me today.

Développé. Again, Ron is at my side. *I am pointing my foot,* I want to holler, but he doesn't notice that. "Do not sacrifice correct placement for a high extension," he says, placing a hand on each of my hips. "Yes!" he cries. "Perfect!" I exhale quietly.

Later I pull off sweaty leg warmers, then grab one of Nana's threadbare towels from the *barre* to wipe my face, forehead, neck. Ron is staring out the window.

"Dancing must be your *life*," he says suddenly.

I follow Peter to the rosin box, nudge my elbow into his side, but he doesn't smile or even acknowledge me. Nana's right. Peter is too serious.

"Pressure will be far, far greater at the National Ballet School than anything you have experienced in my class," Ron warns. "You must be prepared to give up *everything* for your art." He turns from the window and lowers his voice so I can barely hear him. "But the rewards," he grins, "how sweet they are!"

I'm just beginning to wonder why we're getting all this free advice when Ariane turns from the *barre* and walks toward me. Her shiny black hair is tied back into a perfect knot. Unlike me, she isn't perspiring or even breathing hard. As a matter of fact, she looks as if she just stepped out of a magazine ad for Dance-Along leotards. She makes me sick.

Ariane is about four inches taller than me, so I am forced to look up when she says, very sweetly, "You're not thinking of going to the NBS audition, are you, Kate?" Ariane is one of those people who smiles with her mouth closed.

"I . . . I'm . . . not sure."

"It could be bad for your ego," she snorts, gliding

past me to the center of the studio. She proceeds to slide into an exquisite split while I stand there not knowing which way to turn, where to look, how to keep the tears from coming.

Sometimes I wish I had the nerve to tell people what I really think. *Ariane*, I would say, pointing my finger at her lovely nostril, *you are a disgusting human being.* Then I would tell her I hope she breaks her beautiful neck right in the middle of her audition. I would finish up by saying we all know the only reason she will probably make NBS is that her mother is a big shot in the dance world.

We do turns together, then turns alone. Peter is learning to do a *tour en l'air.* He jumps into the air, does a complete turn while he's up there, and lands in fifth. He is determined to get it right, and even though I think he looks terrific on the second try, he and Ron aren't satisfied until about the tenth. Meanwhile, my pal Ariane doesn't waste a minute. Off to the side of the studio, she does a series of *fouetté* turns.

"Bravo!" Ron calls to her when she is finished and smiling.

But even Ron admits that my *pirouettes* are super today. My shoulders aren't twisted, I have a solid *relevé* on the supporting foot, and I spot as if I had been born spotting.

Late in the afternoon I collapse onto a narrow wooden bench in the dressing room. I close my eyes. There is no appropriate way to describe the tingly feeling I have after a good class. It must be the way a swimmer feels after a strenuous swim, or a football player after scoring a touchdown. And the harder I have worked, the more exhilarated I feel. Lots of times I could start class all over again.

"Something wrong, Kate?" Ariane Dukowsky is rubbing her back against my locker. *Go away,* I want to tell her, *before I shove you in the locker and throw away the key.* "That Peter," she whistles softly, "he's *some* dancer—and cute, too."

"I guess so." I am nonchalant.

"The San Francisco Ballet is in town." Ariane unclips her tortoiseshell barrette, and jet black hair falls straight to her shoulders. "My mother has two tickets, and I'm going to invite Peter. Of course, he is a little young for me, but he'll come. I know he will."

It's a good thing I'm such a controlled person— because right now I would relish jumping on Ariane. Peter's *my* friend, I'd let her know with a punch in the nose. Such a pity! Ariane's nose would be bandaged and bleeding for the next two months. Poor thing could never audition for the National Ballet School in that shape. On the other hand, Peter and I would sail through our tryouts and we'd be together, dancing, for the rest of our days. . . .

"What did you say, Kate?" She is still standing there, smiling at me.

I sit up straight and bend both knees to my chest. "Ariane," I sigh, "I've been wondering about something."

"What's that?"

"Um . . . well, never mind." I shake my head from side to side.

"Oh," she bends toward me, "tell me!"

"I shouldn't."

"Please!" Now she's begging for it.

"Well," I begin slowly, "it's that pimple on your nose . . ." Her hand automatically covers the entire (unblemished) nose. "If I were you, I'd be sure to wait until it clears before inviting Peter Robinson anywhere. I happen to know how he feels about older girls with pimples, and let's just say, Ariane, it could be bad for your ego."

8

"I'll walk you home," Peter suggests after class.

"Are you crazy?" I pull the navy blue ski hat over my ears. "We'll be buried alive in this snow."

"Come on, *prima donna*," he says. "I want to show you how to pack a snowball."

"Maybe we should hitch a ride, with *her*." A black station wagon is parked at the curb directly in front of the academy. A tall, mustached chauffeur smiles mechanically as Ariane slides gracefully into the back seat. On top of everything else, the princess happens to be quite rich.

"Yuk." Peter tweaks his nose with two fingers. "Snob."

We start the long trek up Riverside Drive, the wind howling gray-white snow all around us. I imagine for a minute that Peter and I are trapped in a huge tent, one that shuts out the noises, the colors, the commotion of the city. I squint. The world around us is so blanched I can barely make out the line of apartment buildings along the Drive, and it is impossible to figure out where the curbs begin and the sidewalks end.

I turn around and push my back against the wind. Anything to keep upright. Peter is having much more success at that than I. Tracking a narrow footpath, he happily plows ahead, then retraces his steps to rescue me from my latest flop.

"I thought you were a lot tougher than this," he teases, pulling me to a standing position.

"I am. I'm tough." Very suddenly it dawns on me that Peter is missing a great opportunity. What a romantic setup! Right this minute he could be lifting my chin tenderly, the way they do in those old movies. He could be kissing my ruby lips. . . .

"I hate Ariane Dukowsky," I announce.

"She's a good dancer," Peter answers.

I try to sound casual. "I think she's got a crush on you."

Peter screws up his mouth. "Yuk," he says again.

There! I knew Peter wouldn't love Ariane. He's saving his love for me. *Kiss me, kiss me,* I want to shout.

"How is Mr. Schumacher these days?" Peter asks. "Does he still like living with you?"

"I guess so. You know something, Peter? I really like him." Every time I open my mouth to say something, a gob of snow blows in. Kissing would have to be easier than this.

"He is a nice man," Peter agrees. "My father's law partner says Mr. Schumacher is a 'young thinker' for such an old man."

I stop short. "He is not old! You can tell your father's law partner that just because Mr. Schumacher retired doesn't mean he's old." Boy, am I ever beginning to sound like my grandmother. "Besides," I continue, "he's very smart. Every single day he gets mail from his law firm. They're probably sorry they made him leave."

"Okay. Okay." Peter backs off. "Anyway, what do retired people do all day?"

"I don't know about other retired people," I say defensively, "but I suppose Mr. Schumacher reads a lot and talks to Nana. Also," I add, "he's a terrific cook."

"No kidding?"

"Nana even lets him fix whole dinners," I say, "but only sometimes."

"I thought nobody was allowed in Mrs. Stein's kitchen," Peter comments.

"Special rules for Mr. Schumacher."

Peter wipes wet snow off the side of his face. Watching him makes me wonder if he'll be shaving soon. "Special rules," he repeats. "Now, that sounds suspicious to me."

"Why?"

"Well," he begins, "Mrs. Stein is not the kind of lady who would grant special rules to just anybody who comes along. She must like him an awful lot."

"Of course she likes him. Why else would he be living with us?" I demand.

"It can mean only one thing," he says flatly. "She must be in love."

"Peter Robinson! Are you crazy or just plain nuts?" I shout. "My grandmother is not exactly the falling-in-love type."

Peter grins, as if he had cracked the biggest joke in the world. "Just kidding," he says, but I don't care for his sense of humor, and I push ahead through the snow.

"Wait!" he calls, but I won't wait. Even Peter can't say things like that . . . Nana in love. . . .

A wad of snow, icy cold, falls into a million pieces off the back of my neck. I whip around in surprise and another hits my left cheek.

"Why, you . . ." I sputter, wiping my face and my mouth.

Peter is laughing boldly. Crouching down, I pretend to fix my boot, then bolt toward him with a fistful of snow. It misses altogether. Peter is now hysterical. I make another snowball. Aim! Fire! It lands at my feet in humiliating white splinters.

"You just don't have the knack." He approaches so fast I don't have a chance to realize it's a trick.

"Peter, no!" I fall backward and we are rolling in the snow. I squirm and laugh, screech and cough. "Cold! Ach! Uncle! I hate you!"

"Take it back," he snickers, pinning my arms over my head.

"Never!" I spray a mouthful of snow into his smiling face.

Then it happens. Like in the movies and my dreams, and like I had always planned it. Peter kisses me. On the mouth. My eyes pop open. Sweet Peter.

We don't exactly linger. About two seconds later we are brushing the snow off our clothes. I don't have the nerve to look him in the eye. I don't have the courage to take his hand as we continue, in silence, up the Drive.

Ninety-fifth Street. Ninety-sixth Street. Ninety-seventh Street. I clear my throat to say something but there isn't anything to say. Ninety-eighth Street. "I'm sorry," he mumbles. "Are you mad?"

I shake my head. *You've got it all wrong,* I want to tell him. *You're supposed to be glad you kissed me, sorry only that it took you so long to get around to it. . . .*

We round the corner onto 109th Street. I hold my watch under the haze of light from the streetlamp. "Six-thirty!" I whistle. "My grandmother is going to kill me, it's so late." I dig the toe of my boot into the snow. *How about it,* I would like to whisper in his ear, *how about one more kiss—for the road?* Instead I say, "She hates it when I'm irresponsible. Why don't you come upstairs so I don't get a lecture?"

Peter hesitates, then smiles.

We stand in separate corners of the wood-paneled elevator while it grinds to the third floor. Pinky is lurking in the foyer when I open the door. "You're in big trouble," she informs me. "Hi, Peter!"

"Is that Kate?" Nana rushes toward us. "Where have you been, young lady? We've been worried . . . Peter!" She smiles warmly now. "I should have known you two would show up together—eventually."

"I'm sorry, Nana. I don't know how it got so late." *Guess what,* I want to shout, *Peter kissed me!*

"You know you're supposed to call," she is saying. But I am thinking, *Let's step into the bathroom, Nana, for a private talk. You and I never have our little heart-to-hearts anymore. Mr. Schumacher is always around, or Pinky.*

"Is Peter staying for supper?" Pinky asks.

"Of course," Nana answers. "Peter," she points to the phone, "tell your parents you're invited to dinner."

Tonight we are five around the kitchen table.

"It's good to see you, Peter." Mr. Schumacher smiles.

"It's good to see you, too," Peter says. "How have you been?"

"Just fine! They treat me very well around here." Mr. Schumacher winks but his soft gray eyes follow my grandmother as she ladles out steamy bowls of vegetable soup. "Kate tells me you are quite the accomplished dancer these days," he says.

Peter flushes. "Oh, not really," he protests. "But she tells *me* you're a swell cook!"

Mr. Schumacher laughs.

"His chocolate chip cookies are best," Pinky declares. "I even brought some to Miss Falk, to soften her up before my lesson." She giggles.

"Did it work?" Peter asks.

"Well . . ." she shrugs.

"Let's just say Pinky's heart isn't in her piano lessons," I explain to Peter.

"Let's just say," Nana corrects, "if Pinky practiced a little more and complained a little less, her lessons would be a lot more pleasant for all of us."

"What about those famous cookies?" asks Peter. "When do I get to try them?"

"How about tonight!" Pinky turns to Mr. Schumacher. "Won't you please make a batch—for Peter?"

"We'll all help," I say. "Remember what happened the last time I helped, Mr. Schumacher?"

"How could I forget?" he laughs.

"Please!" Pinky repeats.

Mr. Schumacher nods. "I would be honored."

9

Mr. Schumacher gets to work right after dinner. While Pinky and I are busy jamming the kitchen counters with sugar and flour, chocolate bits and mixing bowls, Nana ties a scruffy blue apron around his belly. Peter appoints himself the single-handed cleanup committee. Then we hang around to watch — the mixing and stirring, the pouring and measuring. Mr. Schumacher explains everything he is doing, and soon the delicious-sweet baking smell is everywhere.

"Mmmmm . . . I can practically taste them already." I inhale deeply.

"Are they done yet? *Now* are they done?" Pinky keeps asking.

Finally, the last cookies come out of the oven and we pounce on our proud baker. "Now *you* sit," Nana tells him. She has piled the soft, warm cookies onto a plate and she puts it, along with the half gallon container of milk, in the center of the kitchen table.

"These are incredible!" Peter exclaims. "I've never tasted better cookies."

"Me neither," Pinky agrees.

"Scrumptious," Nana smacks her lips.

"You ought to be in business, Mr. Schumacher," declares Peter, his mouth full of cookie.

"What did you have in mind?" Mr. Schumacher pours himself, then Peter, a second glass of milk.

"What else," says Peter as he leans across the table and waves a cookie under Mr. Schumacher's nose, "the chocolate chip cookie business!"

"Oh. The cookie business." Mr. Schumacher gets this silly smirk on his face, as if he were trying to humor Peter.

"Peter's right," I declare. "The cookie business is a terrific idea."

"You all flatter me," Mr. Schumacher says modestly. "You know, I made up this recipe myself. I reconstructed it from a fabulous dessert my mother used to bake."

"In the old country?" I ask.

He nods. "When I was a little boy, long before I went to school, I loved to watch my mother bake. She let me help with elementary details and we would pass the time making up stories, singing songs . . . it seems like a hundred years ago."

"So, how did you figure out the chocolate chip recipe?" Nana asks.

"Trial and error." Mr. Schumacher smiles. "Over the years I have managed to overcook cookies, and undercook them. I have thrown away cookies that were too buttery or too salty, chewy cookies that were too sweet, and hard-as-rock cookies that tasted simply foul. But I happen to be a little persistent," he winks in the direction of my grandmother, "so I kept plugging away."

"Why *don't* you go into business," I say, "now that they're perfect."

"Ach, Kate. I'm no businessman. I'm a lawyer, a *retired* lawyer. The world doesn't think I'm fit to work anymore." Mr. Schumacher suddenly sounds bitter and sarcastic.

"I don't believe my own ears." That's Nana, and she is staring at Mr. Schumacher in a very alarming way.

"It's the truth," he tells her.

"Pooh, Max Schumacher!" Her voice is sharp and all of a sudden I have that crummy feeling that the two of them have forgotten anyone else is in the room. "You can just stop feeling so sorry for yourself," Nana declares.

"Forty-five years of my life," he says quietly, "that's what I gave that firm."

"It is a long time." Nana's voice is a shade softer. "And I've already told you what I think of those fine fellows who made you retire. But the fact is, you are finished there."

"Finished," he repeats faintly.

"The way I see it, you have two choices," Nana

says to Mr. Schumacher. "You can continue feeling
sorry for yourself and wind up a cranky old man.
Or you can pull yourself together and, to use your
own words, keep plugging. Which is it going to
be?"

Suddenly Nana pushes her chair from the table
and walks quickly from the room.

Pinky's mouth drops open. My eyes meet Peter's
in silence. Mr. Schumacher quietly excuses himself
and follows Nana out of the kitchen.

"Did I say something wrong?" Peter whispers.

I shrug. "They sure act funny sometimes." I scoop
the last cookie off Nana's flowery plate and hand it
to Peter. "Have a cookie."

I knock softly on her bedroom door. "Nana?" I
turn the knob slowly. "Can I come in?" She is bent
over the ancient sewing machine. Each time her
foot hits the floor pedal, the whole room shakes,
pat-pat-pat, pat-pat-pat. "Nana?"

"Yes, Kate." Finally she looks at me.

"Peter and I were wondering," I begin, "can we
take Whiskers for a walk? Mr. Schumacher shouldn't
be out on a night like this. He might slip on the
ice."

"You'll have to ask Mr. Schumacher."

I gently close the door behind me. Pat-pat-pat,
pat-pat-pat.

"What did she say?" Peter is standing in the dim
hallway.

"She told me to ask Mr. Schumacher." We both

shrug, then I tap on the den door. "Mr. Schu-macher? Are you in there?"

The door opens slowly and Whiskers pushes him-self into the hall. The leather leash dangles between his teeth and he spins around in eager circles, trying to catch his tail. "We were wondering, Mr. Schu-macher," I begin all over again, "if you would like us to walk Whiskers tonight . . ."

Mr. Schumacher pats my head, like I'm some little kid he doesn't even know, then pulls on his duffle coat. "That is very thoughtful, Kate, but I need a bit of fresh air myself." His smile is phony and familiar—the one all grown-ups put on when they're trying to make it seem as if everything were all right.

Pinky is practicing scales in the living room, so Peter and I head for my room. "I ought to go home," he says.

"I wish I could come with you," I tell him. "Ev-eryone's so crabby around here." I slide into a pretty good split in the space between the twin beds. "How many weeks till the audition?" I ask casually.

"Four, I think." Peter grins and I bend my head toward my ankle. "You've decided to audition!" he exclaims.

"I haven't made up my mind for sure."

Peter runs his finger along a row of paperbacks on the bookshelf under the window. Every few books he hesitates, pulls one off the shelf, flips pages, then slips it back in place. "I think you're nuts if you don't try," he tells me for the hundredth time.

And for the hundredth time I tell him, "I'm just not sure I'm good enough." I am standing at the foot of the bed, left leg extended back in *arabesque*.

"That is stupid. Really stupid," he says impatiently. "How are you going to be a dancer if you're afraid to go to an audition?"

"Maybe I don't want to be a dancer," I say angrily. Once the words are out of my mouth, I hear how strange they sound. Almost as if someone else had spoken them.

"As long as I've known you, you've wanted to be a dancer," he accuses.

"I know," I sigh.

"Well, here is your big chance." His voice is logical and calm.

But suddenly I don't want to talk about ballet. "Peter," I whisper, "do you think my grandmother and Mr. Schumacher have stopped talking to each other?"

"I doubt it," he answers. "They like each other too much for that."

"Here we go again," I groan. "You're the guy who thinks my *grandmother* is in love."

"Yup."

"What makes you so sure?"

"I can just tell," he says. Such confidence! "It's the way they look at each other—or don't look at each other."

"You happen to be wrong," I inform Peter Robinson.

"So *what* if they like each other?" His face is so close to mine that we are practically knocking noses. "What does that have to do with you?"

"Liking and loving are two different things," I point out. "Besides," I say, taking one step backward, "it has everything to do with me!"

"You know what?" He steps toward me. "I think you're a little on the selfish side." His eyes narrow menacingly and those long auburn bangs swing from side to side.

"I am not! I am not selfish!"

Peter turns away and slowly takes his ski parka off the doorknob. "Maybe you're just immature," he mutters.

"Where are you going?" I follow him to the front foyer.

"Home." He zips the jacket in a single, unfriendly motion.

"Are you angry?"

"Nope." He shakes his head and opens the door to the public hallway. "Thank your grandmother for dinner," he calls over his shoulder.

"Bye." I feel like slamming the door behind him, but of course I don't. I'll save that for the next time he makes me mad.

10

"Peter thinks he's so smart," I tell Nana the next morning at breakfast.

She puts the family-size box of cornflakes on the kitchen table, and a green bowl in front of me. "Why is Peter so smart?" she asks.

"He thinks he's some big shot judge of people . . . people falling in love and stuff like that."

"Umhmmmmm." She sits in the chair next to me.

I turn the cereal box upside down. Hundreds of cornflakes tumble into the bowl. "He claims he can just *tell* when certain people are in love. Isn't that stupid, Nana?"

Pinky shuffles into the kitchen, her green flannel nightgown dragging along the floor. She rubs her eyes. "Nana," she yawns, "can I go sleigh riding?"

"Right this minute?" Nana hurries to the refrigerator and pours a glass of orange juice. Fresh-squeezed. "We're having breakfast now. Afterward Kate will take you to Riverside Park."

"Nana," I moan, "that's for little kids."

She looks at me with a warning eye. "I think you can do this little favor for your sister."

"What about Mr. Schumacher?" I suggest. "Maybe he would like to go sleigh riding."

Nana waves a basket of warm rolls in the air and says, "Mr. Schumacher went to Brooklyn late last night."

"Brooklyn?"

Nana sits again. She begins to fold a paper napkin into perfect even squares. Then she unfolds each square and flattens the napkin across the table. "He is visiting friends."

"I didn't know he had friends in Brooklyn," Pinky comments as she smears raspberry jam across the top of her roll.

"Apparently he does." Nana chips away at the words.

"How come he has to go see them in the middle of a snowstorm—and in the middle of the night?" I ask. "Isn't that a little crazy, Nana?"

But then I remember how our little cookie party ended last night. Maybe they did stop talking to each other, just as I suspected. Maybe Mr. Schumacher went to Brooklyn because he doesn't like us anymore. Maybe he wants to find another place to live!

Nana is folding the napkin into squares again and she doesn't look very happy. "Eat your breakfast," she says quietly.

"I'm not hungry." I wrap my arm around her shoulder, kiss the wrinkles in her forehead. "I love you," I whisper. Louder, I say, "Aren't you ready yet, Pinky? You're the one who's supposed to be dying to go sleigh riding."

Riverside Park. The sun is brilliant, the snow packed so tight it creaks and crunches beneath our feet. Pinky twirls around and around, her cheeks shiny and crimson from the cold. I lag behind, pulling the little wooden sled by its worn rope, the same rope Grampa used to knot together every winter.

"I'll bet you there's no school tomorrow," Pinky sings. "No school! No school!"

"Umhmmmmmm."

"We can fool around all day," she tells me, as if I'm her best friend.

"Umhmmmmmm."

"You're in a rotten mood," she informs me, as if I didn't already know that.

"Mind your own business," I grumble.

"Grouch." She yanks the sled from me and stomps ahead. Insulted. Wounded. It's amazing how easy it is to hurt someone when you don't really mean to.

"Pinky!" I call.

"What?" She slows down but doesn't look at me. My punishment.

"Do you ever wonder about Nana?" I ask the back of her ski hat.

"Wonder what?"

I've nearly caught up to her. "Well, do you ever wonder what goes on in her head?"

Pinky stops short and whirls around. "What are you talking about?"

"I was just wondering," I say slowly, "what if there was someone else in Nana's life?"

"So?"

"What if, for example, there was another person, besides you and me, that she liked?"

"So?" she repeats.

"And what if that person began to take up all her time? Where would that leave us, Pinky?"

"It would leave us just the same as always," she answers simply.

"You're wrong about that," I tell her. "It would leave us very much in the way." I feel my throat getting tighter. "It would leave us very much out of the picture—Nana's picture, that is . . . "

"I wish you would speak English." Pinky is exasperated. "I still don't know what you're talking about."

"Do you think," I sigh, "that Nana and Mr. Schumacher like each other?"

"Of course they do." She smiles brightly.

"I mean *like* each other. The way Nana and Grampa liked each other, or our parents."

Now she eyes me like some doubting puppy. "Are you asking me if I think they *love* each other?"

I knew it! I knew I couldn't talk to a baby like Pinky. Just like Peter, she doesn't see that some people like each other and other people are in love.

Pinky suddenly clutches my hand and propels us to the nearest snow-coated tree. We lean against it, then slide down to sit on the hard, cold ground.

"You think they're in love?" She half whispers, half shrieks.

"I never said that."

Her eyes are wide and sparkly and excited. "Do you think they'll get *married?*"

"What a stupid thing to say."

"Wow!" She grabs my shoulders. "Wow!"

I unglue myself from her annoying grasp and stand up. "Forget it," I say, brushing a layer of snow off my rear end. "Let's just forget the whole thing."

For the next two hours I am an outsider. I trace and retrace my steps across the top of Sled Hill. There must be a million kids out here today, and they come in all sizes but mostly boxy shapes in their colorful snow outfits. One by one they whiz by, careless and happy.

It isn't fair, what's happening in my life. First Mr. Schumacher thinks he ought to come live with us. Then my good friend Peter (ha!) decides Nana and Mr. Schumacher are falling in love. Next thing I know, Mr. Schumacher is traipsing off to Brooklyn in the middle of the night. Then I find out my own sister is thrilled at the notion that Nana could get married.

"Kate?"

"Peter!" I cry out, much too loud. "What are you doing on Sled Hill?" I mean to sound aloof and angry, but as usual I'm so glad to see him.

"Your grandmother said you were here," he answers. "Look, I even brought this beat-up sled, and some Nestlés—a peace offering," he adds. "Where is Pinky?"

"Out there." I point to the bottom of the hill. "She's a real daredevil," I say. "I don't know where she gets it."

Peter stuffs his hands into his pants pockets. With the toe of his all-weather boot, he hacks away at a small mound of snow. "Listen," he begins, "I had no right to say those things about your grandmother and Mr. Schumacher. And about you. I'm sorry."

"Forget it," I say. "I'm sick of talking about it."

"I shouldn't have said any of it," he insists. "It's none of my business."

"Peter Robinson!" I exclaim. "If you're my friend, then it is your business. Friends are supposed to share their problems."

He sighs. "There you go again, saying it's a problem. *Why* is it a problem?"

"I don't know." I want to shout, but my voice is a whisper. "Maybe because it changes everything."

"Hi, Peter!" Pinky clumps toward us. "Watch me!" she yells. "Watch!" She picks up her sled, flops onto it, pushes off with her feet, then flies straight to the bottom of the run.

Peter faces me. "What does it change?"

"What are you, some kind of psychiatrist?" I say.

"Yeah," he answers, rubbing a fake beard. "I'm your shrink." He lowers his voice about seventeen

notches. "Young lady," he jokes, "you must tell me
what the problem is."

"Well, Doctor," I begin, "with Mr. Schumacher in
the apartment, it's impossible to walk around without any clothes!"

"I see," he answers, still rubbing his chin. "Well,
at least you won't catch cold!"

"Also, it's a terrible thing the way Mr. Schumacher makes us eat those chocolate chip cookies
all the time."

"I see," he repeats. "It's good you don't have any
teeth, or you would have many cavities, no?"

"Cut it out!" I laugh. "This happens to be serious."

"If you ask me," he says, going back to his own
voice, "I think you should stop worrying so much."

"Maybe," I answer. "Anyway, I think Mr. Schumacher ran away from home last night. Nana's feel-
ings are hurt, I can tell."

"Mr. Schumacher is not the run-away-from-home
type," Peter assures me. "Besides, he couldn't get
very far in this snow." Peter pulls his sled to the
start-off point at the top of the hill. "I will now
demonstrate—*voilà!*" He secures the splintery-looking
sled with one foot. "Come on, Kate," he calls.

"Not me." I shake my head. "I hate sleigh riding."

"You what?"

"I hate it!" I repeat emphatically.

"How could you hate something that's so much
fun?" He is incredulous.

"I'm chicken," I admit. "I even hate swings. They
make me nauseous. Besides, what if I fall off and
break a leg?"

"You can't break your leg on a little kid's sled,"
he insists. "Watch!" He jumps on, head and stomach first, shouting, "Timber!"

I force myself to watch him zigzag down the long
graceful hill, faster, faster. I can picture Peter break-
ing his neck, let alone a leg. Showoff. Finally, he is
standing at the bottom, holding up his hand in a V
for victory salute.

His jeans are powder-white from the snow, and
even though Peter is far and away the biggest kid
down there, I'm convinced he is also the cutest.

It's nearly dark when we pull our sleds into the
big old building on Riverside Drive. I rub my hands
together and blow on them. Pinky does too. I stamp
crusty snow off my boots and wait for her to copy
me. She does.

"Will you come upstairs?" I ask Peter.

He glances at his watch. "For a few minutes," he
answers. "My parents are taking me to the ballet
tonight."

"Lucky you," I sigh. "I wish we could afford it."
As I say the words a picture pops into my head. I
am a ballerina, beautiful and rich and quite famous.
I am waving to my fans as I step into a sleek black
limousine in front of the Metropolitan Opera House.
Ariane Dukowsky's mustached chauffeur drives me
away. . . .

"My father says," Peter is grumbling, "as long as
it's someone else's kid up there, the ballet is a fine
cultural experience." He looks disgusted.

"We're home!" Pinky announces as we shed ski parkas in the front foyer.

"Hang your wet jackets on the railing in the bathroom," Nana calls from the kitchen. "Pinky, take the first bath. You girls must be freezing."

Peter and I head for the kitchen.

One thing's for sure. Around here there are always plenty of surprises. Surprise number one: Mr. Schumacher is back. Surprise number two: He and Nana are bent over a yellow legal pad at the kitchen table. Their chairs are so close that their shoulders nearly touch.

I look at Peter and roll my eyes to the top of my head. He raises his eyebrows, then shrugs as if to say, *What did I tell you?*

I clear my throat. "Hello, everybody."

Neither one looks up. "How was the sledding?" Nana asks.

"Okay," I say. "Fine."

Silence.

"Peter is here," I say, slightly irritated.

They raise their heads to acknowledge him, and I strain my neck to see the scratchings on the yellow pad in front of them. "What are you doing?" I ask as casually as possible.

"Mr. Schumacher is working on a project," Nana says, and she is practically beaming.

I swear, sometimes I just can't figure her out. Now she behaves as if nothing had ever happened—no fights, no walking out in the middle of the night. Peter's right. I worry too much. Nobody is listening anyway.

"There!" Mr. Schumacher draws a red circle around a group of numbers, then waves the paper in the air.

"What is it?" Peter asks, kicking off his drippy boots.

"You tell them," Nana says to Mr. Schumacher. She folds her hands on the table and presses her lips together as if she were holding in some big secret.

"What's going on?" I demand.

"I have been doing some serious thinking," Mr. Schumacher begins. "Last night Peter suggested something which, at the time, seemed ridiculous to me. But hours later I was turning and tossing in my bed. A little voice inside my head kept reprimanding me. 'Max, you're feeling sorry for yourself,' the voice admonished. 'It makes you old.'

"Suddenly," he continues, "I found myself full of energy and raring to go. I got dressed, then took a taxi all the way to Brooklyn where I met with a friend, or rather a business acquaintance. We tossed this idea back and forth, and one thing led to another. Now I've decided." Mr. Schumacher beams, as if he had just invented the electric light or something.

"Decided *what?*"

Mr. Schumacher inhales deeply. Then very slowly he says, "I am going into the chocolate chip cookie business."

Five seconds of total silence.

"Terrific!" Peter practically shouts.

"I have you to thank," Mr. Schumacher tells him. "It was your idea."

Peter looks down toward his yellow sweat socks.
"Nah, it's just that your cookies *taste* so good."

"All those compliments went straight to my head,"
Mr. Schumacher answers. "Then again," he adds,
"if the whole plan fails, I can always say it was
Peter's crummy old idea."

Suddenly Peter extends his hand and he and Mr.
Schumacher shake. "Good luck, Mr. Schumacher."

Sweet Peter. He always does the right thing. I
reach for Mr. Schumacher's free hand. "Good luck,
Mr. Schumacher," I mimic. "What are you going to
call your business?"

"We'll put our heads together and think of something catchy," he answers. "Also, we will need a
distribution plan. How will people know about the
cookies? Word of mouth? Fancy advertising? And
how much will we charge?"

If anyone were to ask me right this minute how
old Mr. Schumacher is, I would answer, *Why, there's
a young man if I've ever seen one! Just look at the sparkle
in his eye, the proud way he throws back his shoulders.
Just listen to the music in his voice. . . .*

"So," he is saying, "we have a lot of work ahead
of us."

"Can we help?" I ask.

"You bet," Nana tells me. "It wouldn't be possible without you children."

I watch her eyes. Nana says she had lovely violet-
colored eyes when she was a young girl, but right
now they are the softest shade of blue, and I can't
imagine anything prettier in the whole world.

"I have a sneaky suspicion," Nana continues, "that inside a couple of weeks this place is going to look more like a cookie factory than an apartment."

Mr. Schumacher grins at me. "Now what do you think of your grandmother — offering her kitchen for such a crazy venture! Isn't she something special?"

"She's the best."

Then Pinky comes in, scrubbed and warm from her bath. I must admit she looks pretty cute in the new sweat shirt from Macy's. Hooded, zippered, and bright red, it is the fourth-grade rage at P.S. 62. "What's going on?" she asks.

"We're going into business." Peter flips the hood onto her head.

"When do we start?" I ask.

Mr. Schumacher and Nana turn to each other. If I didn't know better, I would swear they were romantically inclined, and really, it's a little nauseating. Without even glancing my way, Mr. Schumacher answers the question. "How about right now?"

11

It's hard to believe how things change in our house from one day to the next. On Monday Nana and Mr. Schumacher take a long subway ride to Queens. They don't get home until after dark, happily reporting they have just bought nearly one hundred pounds of flour and butter, sugar, eggs, and chocolate.

"A hundred pounds!" I shriek.

"We got everything wholesale," Mr. Schumacher says.

"If we buy in bulk," Nana explains, "it's a lot cheaper." She ties an apron—the one with yellow chickens on the pockets—around her waist. "Dinner will be late," she apologizes.

"When do we start baking?" asks Pinky.

"Mr. Klein, the man who sold us the ingredients, guarantees a delivery tomorrow," answers Mr. Schumacher. "He gave his word that his trucks are moving despite the snowstorm."

"How many cookies will we bake, to start?" I ask.

I must admit I'm getting awfully excited about Mr. Schumacher's new business. Imagine having a cookie factory right in your own apartment! Mr. Schumacher will get rich. Maybe he'll even be rich enough to keep me in those expensive toe shoes. That way Nana can't complain that my dancing is unaffordable. Maybe he'll even be rich enough to take me to the ballet once in a while ... and of course, he won't be feeling useless and old.

After a picnic-style dinner of salami sandwiches and coleslaw, Mr. Schumacher arranges four yellow legal pads and four number two pencils around the kitchen table. He says this is how it's done in a law office. We take our places, and he instructs each of us to write down any suggestions we might have for the business.

At the top of a clean sheet of paper, I write:

KATE'S SUGGESTIONS FOR MR. SCHUMACHER'S
CHOCOLATE CHIP COOKIE BUSINESS

1. Name of business (Something catchy)
2. Who bakes? (I do)
3. Who cleans up? (Pinky)
4. Who will buy the cookies? (Everyone in New York)
5. How much money should we charge? (Fifty dollars a cookie!)

❖   ❖   ❖

"This meeting is called to order." Mr. Schumacher bangs his gavel (actually, it's a small hammer from the toolbox Nana keeps in the linen closet) on the wooden table.

"Thank you for attending," he begins formally, "and for wanting our business to get off to a good start. The first thing on today's agenda is to name our cookie venture. Suggestions, please!"

"How about the Chewy Chip Factory?" Pinky smiles hopefully.

Mr. Schumacher carefully writes it down under the heading "Business Name."

"Mrs. Stein?" he says.

"You won't laugh?"

"Only if it's hilarious," Mr. Schumacher answers.

"What do you think of Max's Makeshift Cookie House?" she says slowly.

"I like it!" I exclaim.

"Me too," says Pinky.

Nana grins. Mr. Schumacher bangs his gavel on the table for the second time. "Time to vote," he says. "I vote aye."

"Aye!" say Pinky and I in a single breath.

Mr. Schumacher pounds the gavel one more time. "It is unanimous. Max's Makeshift Cookie House!"

Then we all get up and hug each other. What fun this is going to be—and democratic. Mr. Schumacher sure knows how to include people in his affairs. Too bad we have to go to school tomorrow. I would love to be here when Mr. Klein's supersnowplow of a truck pulls up at the front of our building and unloads one hundred pounds of cookie ingredients. The neighbors will go crazy, trying to figure out what's going on.

"Next on the agenda," Mr. Schumacher is saying, "we need to talk about an advertising policy."

"What's that?" asks Pinky.

"We have to let people know we're in business, right?" he answers.

Pinky puts her fist under her chin, then says, "We can advertise in *The New York Times!*"

"That's an excellent suggestion," Mr. Schumacher assures her, "but I'm afraid we don't have the funds—not yet."

"Oh."

"The important thing," Nana adds, "is to advertise cheaply."

"We can put signs in the elevator," I suggest.

"Good!" Mr. Schumacher prints "Elevator signs" on his pad.

"But we have to expand beyond this apartment building," Nana insists. "Mr. Schumacher's cookies are so good the whole city should hear about them."

"Hip, hip, hurrah!" Pinky sings.

"I'll ask Pat Mandella—she's class president now—to pass the word around in school," I say. "And *I'll* pass the word in ballet class. Instead of Girl Scout cookies, we get to sell Mr. Schumacher's!"

"We need a press release," Nana says thoughtfully, "to let people know what we're selling. I can write it, and Pinky, our resident artist, will draw a design—our logo." Nana smiles at my sister. "Also, you can be in charge of running them off at the photocopy center on Broadway."

Our meeting lasts more than an hour. Somewhere around nine o'clock Pinky drops her head across folded arms, and two minutes later she is sound asleep, her breath coming in even, rhythmic patterns. That's when Mr. Schumacher adjourns the first official meeting of Max's Makeshift Cookie House.

"I don't know, Peter," I complain, wrapping the long woolen scarf around my neck. "Less than a month till the audition, and look at me—a basket case. My stomach is in knots and I can't eat. I can't fall asleep at night and I'm convinced by the way Ron's been picking on me that my dancing gets worse by the day."

"I've told you a million times," Peter answers. "He *isn't* picking on you. He's trying to *help* you—because he thinks you're good."

"But am I good enough?" I sigh.

"You're just getting nervous," Peter assures me.

"Of course I'm nervous! Aren't you?"

He shrugs. "Nope. I can't afford to be."

"But it's more than nerves," I continue. "I think these NBS auditions are beginning to make me a little sick."

"Too sick for a soda at Jake's?" he grins. Sometimes Peter makes me so angry. He jokes when I want to be serious. He treats the most important day of his life—March 16—as if it were no more important than a trip to the neighborhood soda fountain. How can he be so cool?

We walk down the two murky flights from the ballet school. The late-afternoon sun makes long cold shadows on Broadway. Saturday shoppers whoosh by, carrying colorful shopping bags, pushing baby strollers, and mostly looking as if they needed to start the weekend all over again.

Jake's is a run-down but homey little candy store near the corner of Eighty-eighth Street. It is squished in between a gourmet treat center and a fancy-looking health food store. Jake himself must be a hundred years old, and the story goes that he refused to sell his store for a million dollars, even though the rest of the block is being renovated into a glamorous shopping plaza.

A narrow and cluttered aisle leads to the back. We sit on two of the three wobbly stools.

"Yeah?" The teenager behind the counter looks as if he wouldn't know a bottle of shampoo if one fell on him.

"Orange juice, please."

"Root beer and a rare hamburger," says Peter.

I put an elbow on the counter and rest my head on my hand. "You see," I say slowly, "it's finally beginning to dawn on me that I'm never going to be a star."

"How do you know?" Peter turns the bottle of ketchup upside down and barricades it with little cubes of sugar.

"I *know*. Sometimes you just feel these things. My

grandmother always tells me I push myself too much," I continue, "and I think she's right."

"Yeah, but she never told you to *quit*." Peter flicks two fingers against the side of the bottle and spins it around and around.

"It wouldn't be quitting. I am not a quitter."

He turns to face me. "Then why won't you audition?"

"I thought you were my friend, Peter." I shake my head. "You act as if you wouldn't talk to me again if I decided not to audition."

"I *am* your friend," he insists. "That's why I think you should audition. You'll never get anywhere if you don't go through with this."

"So what," I mumble, thinking what a disaster it would be if Peter and that rat Ariane went on to the National Ballet School without me. Why, I'd be nowhere. Nowhere! Peter would be too busy and too proud to bother with a flunky named Kate, and the two of them would dance off, never looking back, never feeling the tiniest little bit sorry for me. . . .

"Are you sure you want to be a dancer?" Peter is beginning to sound slightly disgusted with me.

I blow the paper off the straw the greasy kid put in front of me. I wish I could think of something brilliant to say.

"I don't know what you're so afraid of," he tells me, and his voice is kinder.

"The way I see it," I begin, "the difference between you and me, and between creepy Ariane and

me, is that the two of you are willing to give up
everything to dance."

Peter takes a long strawful of root beer. He stares
ahead, at the ancient grill that sizzles his hamburger
and the opaque plastic cups piled in the sink. Right
this minute he looks much older, like someone too
wise and sophisticated to be associating with a kid
like me.

"Well?" I say. "Aren't I right?"

He smiles slightly, as if he'd just awakened from a
pleasant dream. "It's my life," he says simply.

Peter douses his hamburger with extras. Extra
pickles from the tinny bowl on the counter, extra
onions, and about a pound of ketchup. He carefully
cuts it in half. Then, like the gentleman I always
knew he was, he hands me my share. One thing
about Peter Robinson is he always knows the right
thing to do.

12

MAX'S MAKESHIFT COOKIE HOUSE
370 Riverside Drive
Manhattan

Max Schumacher's old-world recipe
for chocolate chip cookies can't be beat.
Try one and you will never go back
to the packaged variety. Expensive?
They may cost a little more, but
taste one and you'll see why. We use
the best ingredients money can buy.

Place your order today.
You'll wish you placed it yesterday.

We put one of Nana's press releases under each
door in our building. I take a batch to school and

hand them out at lunchtime. Pinky does too, and she brings a bunch to her music school in the Village. I volunteer to circulate flyers on Broadway, but Nana and Mr. Schumacher veto that suggestion on the grounds that girls who stand on street corners have a knack for finding trouble.

Mr. Schumacher's wholesale delivery came right on schedule. When I got home from school that Monday, bulky brown sacks of flour were stacked against the kitchen door. Blocks of butter were crammed every which way in the refrigerator, and bags of sugar, boxes of eggs, and assorted packages were stuffed into the tiled area under the old porcelain sink.

"Where are we going to put everything!" I exclaimed.

Nana was sitting at the kitchen table. She cracked one egg after another into a big glass bowl. "It won't be so bad," she answered. "We just need to get organized."

Mr. Schumacher's sleeves were rolled up over his elbows. He used a long wooden spoon to blend cookie batter in a brand-new, extra-large aluminum pot. "And there's another feature to this business, Kate," he said, pointing to his left bicep. "I'm getting muscles at the ripe old age of seventy-one!"

"Muscles build character." I stuck my forefinger into the batter, smacked my lips loudly. "Delicious!"

"Kate." Nana pointed to the kitchen door. "Out, out, out!"

"Just testing," I called from the hallway, "like they do in the Betty Crocker kitchens."

That was just three weeks ago.

It looks as though Peter was right because the cookie business is really taking off. Mr. Schumacher just may be a businessman, after all! Of course, now the apartment is cluttered and chaotic all the time. If the phone isn't ringing, then it's the doorbell. Orders. Reorders. Orders. More reorders.

If Nana and Mr. Schumacher aren't stirring and mixing and counting out cookies, they're hunched over their long sheets of paper work. Cold suppers have become routine; that is just as well since the taste of chocolate chip cookies seems to be in everything we eat. And even though Nana and Mr. Schumacher keep talking about getting organized, I'm beginning to doubt they ever will.

"If this activity continues, we will have to open our own bakery, with a warehouse!" Mr. Schumacher beams.

"Nonsense," says Nana. "We're doing very nicely right here. Besides," she adds, "the girls couldn't contribute as much if we were working downtown somewhere."

The truth is I love helping out with Max's Makeshift Cookie House. My main job is to hand out the press releases and tell people about the cookies. Publicity, Mr. Schumacher calls it. But I am also allowed to take phone orders and sometimes I pack cookies for a pickup. Mr. Schumacher and Nana are the bakers, and Pinky delivers to customers in

our building. Business must be pretty good because
Mr. Schumacher even bought a pocket calculator to
make the arithmetic easier.

The funny thing is when I'm helping with the
cookies, I actually forget to think about ballet. But
then, when I least expect it, pop! The picture leaps
into my head. I am that famous ballerina, beautiful
and rich. I perform in the sophisticated cities of the
world, but especially in New York where Nana and
the others can come and see me. Me! Dancing
every single day, dancing . . .

"You'll never get anywhere if you don't go through
with this audition." That's what Peter said.

And nasty old Ron isn't being too subtle these
days either. "You missed *two* Thursday classes," he
said accusingly.

"I was baking . . . cookies . . ." I apologized
meekly, but he walked away, and for the rest of
class he never once stopped by to correct me. "Dance
must be your *life*," he had told us that snowy
afternoon.

If only I were a little kid again. Then Nana could
tell me what to do. It's a curious thing with her. For
the unimportant stuff ("Comb your hair!" or "Be
home before dark"), she is so tough. But when it
comes to the really big issues, like the NBS audition, my grandmother has the most annoying way of
letting me make my own decisions.

"Nana!" I have been stalling for an hour. The
French text is open, untouched, to the chapter on
pluperfect. Lounging across my bed, I reach for the

door and call to her. "Nana!" I repeat. "Can you
come here?"

"I'm busy," she replies.

Swell. Too busy with Mr. Schumacher to talk to
her own granddaughter. I fall backward and raise
my legs toward the ceiling. Scissor kicks . . . one
and two. Maybe Peter is right; if I would just
audition, my decision would be made for me. If the
judges select me, I'll go on to the National Ballet
School this summer. If they don't pick me, well . . .

The door opens and Nana comes in brushing a
powdery layer of flour off her hands and onto her
apron. "What's up?" She sits on the edge of my
bed.

"I thought you were busy." There I go again,
saying things that sound so awful the second they're
out of my mouth.

"Never too busy to talk with you." Her tone is
sarcastic but she smiles and I am forgiven.

"I'm in a fix, Nana."

"What kind of fix?" she asks.

"I can't decide what to do about that audition," I
tell her. "I'm just not sure I'm good enough."

"You're afraid you'll be turned down." She says it
as if she were some kind of mind reader.

"That's part of it," I sigh. "The other part is I'm
not even sure I *want* to study at the National Ballet
School. Everybody says it's horribly competitive.
They say the pressure is so great that kids are
always having nervous breakdowns. . . ."

"Kate," she frowns, "wherever did you hear such a ridiculous story?"

I shrug. "Just around."

"But you love your classes," she reminds me.

"I know, but I have a feeling it's kid stuff compared to the National Ballet School."

She nods.

"Peter says," and I stare down at the red plaid quilt on my bed, "maybe I don't want to be a dancer."

Nana makes a little clicking sound with her tongue. "One day you want something, and the next day you don't," she says slowly. "Grown-ups have that problem, too."

"Peter says I'd be a quitter."

"Nonsense!" She looks at me sternly. "Peter's whole life is ballet. He has made a total commitment, and nothing will stand in his way." Nana leans toward me and our faces are very close. "When he auditions on the sixteenth, it's because that's the right thing for *him* to do."

"I'm not a quitter, Nana."

"I know that," she smiles. Using her fingers like a comb, she pushes the hair away from her forehead. The soft white fluff reminds me of the flour from our cookies and the snow before New Yorkers traipse all over it. "And there's something else," she continues. "You may not be ready to audition right now, but it's important to remember you're only twelve years old—not exactly over the hill, even for a ballerina. Peter is a little older, and so is that Ariane girl you keep talking about."

"And what happens when the two of them make the NBS? What happens to *me*, Nana?" I mumble.

Nana takes a deep breath, then lets the air out slowly. "You mean, what happens when the two of them start going places and you're left behind."

I nod.

"It would be hard to take, all right, but you would learn to accept it," she says, very matter-of-fact. "That's no reason for you to audition, Kate."

"You don't understand," I sigh, but I know she does, and she knows it.

"One thing I've learned from all the literature you bring me on being a professional dancer is you don't *have* to study at the National Ballet School at the age of twelve." Nana pauses briefly. "The point is, Kate, all won't be lost if you wait a year or two."

"Wait a year or two . . ." I repeat the words and suddenly they make sense. "Nana," I say softly, "maybe that's the answer—and I never even thought of it. I never even thought about next year."

When she hugs me it feels safe and good, like when I was little. When life was simple. "Sometimes we're so close to a situation that we can't see it clearly," she tells me.

"How will I know if I'm ready next year, Nana?"

"Suppose we take it one year at a time," she says. "It's easier that way."

"So much can happen in a year," I add. "Like with Mr. Schumacher. Who would have thought, even half a year ago, that he'd be living here with us?"

"Certainly not I," she answers thoughtfully.

"Nana," I say, "are you having a good time out there with Mr. Schumacher?"

"I'm having a very nice time."

"Sometimes I wonder if Mr. Schumacher likes me," I tell her.

"Of course he does," she answers quickly. "He happens to be crazy about the two of you—you and Pinky."

"It's just that he's got so many important things on his mind, and maybe he thinks I'm in the way around here."

"In the way!" she exclaims. "There's no such thing as being in the way with your own family."

"I guess I'm still getting used to having an extra person around," I confess. "Probably, I wasn't so nice to him in the beginning."

"It does take getting used to," she agrees. She cups her hand under my chin. "What really counts, though, isn't how many we are, but how we *feel* about each other. Do you understand, Kate?"

"Yes." And then: "Do you think Mr. Schumacher feels like he's a part of our family, Nana?"

"If he's smart, he does." Now she smiles.

I'm supposed to be sleeping like a log. When a girl makes a big decision, like the one I've made tonight, she's supposed to drop into a deep, sweet slumber. Not me. I squirm around for endless hours,

trying to block out thoughts of the National Ballet
School, of Peter and Ariane, of *pirouettes* and *fouetté*
turns.

I visit with Nana quietly in the kitchen when it is
midnight and then when it is one o'clock in the
morning. We don't talk about ballet. In fact, we
don't talk much at all. She makes me warm milk,
which I hate, but she's right. It settles my stomach,
and finally, I sleep.

I dream that I call on Mr. and Mrs. Stuffed Shirt
Robinson.

"You may not remember me," I tell them, "but
I'm Peter's best friend. Kate's the name. We plan to
be married, but not yet. I came here to tell you a
thing or two about your son."

"Oh, dear!" squeaks Mrs. Robinson.

"Peter happens to be a wonderful person!" (I
shout that part.) "He's kind and sensitive, and he
kissed me. He helped Mr. Schumacher get started
in business, and he says the nicest things to my
grandmother to make her feel good. Also, Peter is
the best student at the New York Ballet Academy.
He's going to be a star one day, you'll see!"

Naturally they are stunned. Such raves about
their only son!

"Bring the finest wineglasses," Mrs. Robinson
orders her housekeeper, and the three of us toast
Peter. Then that handsome boy comes in from the
cold. He hugs me and kisses the tip of my ear.
Wow! His parents start to cry and they apologize

for not understanding how much dancing means to him. Then I wake up.

"Mr. Robinson is a creep," I announce at breakfast.
"Kate!"

"It happens to be true," I say, carefully spreading a thin layer of butter on my rye toast. "He won't accept the fact that Peter wants to be a dancer."

"Perhaps," Mr. Schumacher suggests, "he fears Peter's life as a dancer would be too unstable, unpredictable."

"Max!" my grandmother scolds. "The future is always unpredictable." She turns to me. "Knowing Peter, I assume he will audition over his father's objections."

"Yup," I answer and suddenly I feel very proud of Peter, proud to be his friend. "I wish his parents were supportive like you, Nana."

She pours herself, then Mr. Schumacher, a second cup of coffee. I notice she isn't using her crinkly aluminum coffee pot, but the shiny electric one Mr. Schumacher moved down from 14A. "Thanks for the compliment," she says.

Then Mr. Schumacher turns to me and says, "What about you, Kate? Have you made up your mind about the audition?"

I focus my eyes on a small patch of green-flowered wallpaper directly in front of me. "Well," I begin casually, "it looks as if I've decided not to audition."

"That's not fair!" Pinky screeches. "Now I don't get to have a famous sister."

Nana looks at me. "Are you sure?" she asks.

"I think so." I watch the funny way the flowers twist and turn and whirl around each other. "Are you all very disappointed in me?"

"Disappointed!" repeats Mr. Schumacher. "I should say not. It often takes a lot of guts to do what you feel is right."

"And it sure feels right," I sigh.

I bite off a small piece of toast, and another. I eat until there's nothing left, and then I reach for seconds. So, it's that easy. All you have to do is say it, and already you feel better. It doesn't even hurt. *I am not going to audition, and I'm going to live. I am not a quitter, and I still love ballet. I will take class for the rest of my life because I love the way it makes me feel.*

Now there is only one little problem to solve. I need to find a way to tell Peter. I need to make him understand.

13

March is a funny time of year. By now I'm sick and tired of the cold and the leftover snow is just a mess on city streets. The days are getting longer, but it seems like forever until spring, let alone the end of school. Today is typical, wet and cold, and I'm glad to come home. Peter and I trudge up the back stairs to 3C. It's that in-between hour, not quite night, but not daytime either.

"I've never been so tired in my life," I groan when there are eight steps to go.

"Your *pirouettes* were super today," he answers. "Do those on the sixteenth, and the judges will *beg* you to spend the summer at the NBS."

Peter darling, did I forget to tell you? I imagine myself saying. *I've decided not to audition.* Instead I say, "I wonder if the baking is finished for the day."

"Mrs. Stein says business is booming," Peter declares.

"Mr. Schumacher will be a millionaire if this keeps up. People knock on our door all night long for reorders, and we even had to get another phone," I say. "The apartment's a wreck and I'm sick to death of the sweet smell. But it's doing wonders for them . . . for Mr. Schumacher."

Pinky pulls open the front door. "Guess what?" she chirps. "I'm on the payroll! Mr. Schumacher made me a contract and I'm going to earn sixty cents an hour."

"Good for you," I say, wondering why I don't get contracts. "Where is everyone?" I fling my parka toward the couch. It lands in a red heap on the floor.

"Delivering cookies," Pinky answers. "Guess what?" she repeats. Before I get a chance to guess what, she blurts out the news that Mother's Best Bakery wants to start selling our cookies. "We're having a business meeting tonight, to discuss it," she adds importantly.

Peter whistles. "Bakery sales, business meetings . . ." He collapses into the club chair. "This is beginning to sound very impressive," he says.

"You sure look beat." Pinky crosses her legs and sits on the floor in front of him. I head for the shower, but don't miss her next question. "Are you going to be a famous dancer, Peter?"

It's incredible to me that my sister is so immature she can ask a question like that. But as I close the bathroom door, I find myself hoping that Pinky—in her immature way—will spill the beans about my National Ballet School decision. What are sisters for if they can't do you a little favor once in a while?

Five minutes later. I check into the living room in a white button-down shirt and fresh jeans. I sit on the couch across from Peter and start to brush my hair. A quick study of his face, and I know Pinky has not spilled any beans, or done me any favors.

"Your hair's getting long," Peter tells me. "Perfect dancer's hair."

It's good Peter is beginning to notice things about the way I look. Just last week he told me I have a dancer-lean body. Now I try to catch Pinky's attention, indicate with my eyes that it's time for her to leave. She doesn't budge. Instead, she sits there hugging her knees, eyes stuck on Peter. And it's no wonder! Even slouched down in the old blue chair, Peter has a way of looking terrific. How, I wonder, can a person look so comfortable and so perfectly controlled at the same time?

"You know," he is saying, "the two of you don't look a bit like sisters."

Pinky and I face each other. "Of course we don't look alike," I say solemnly. "You see, we *found* Pinky—in a picnic basket in Riverside Park. She was waving to us with her pinky. That's how she got her name. . . ."

"Cut it out," she warns.

"We couldn't just leave her there," I continue. "She was such a pathetic little thing."

Pinky giggles, putting an end to my story. Then she turns to Peter. "I look just like my mother," she says simply.

"She does," I agree. I twist around to the big oval mirror behind the couch and start to braid my hair. Secretly I can watch Peter in the mirror, and from this angle I can see he is watching me, too. "There!" I fold over the last third of hair halfway down my back, then wind a rubber band around the braid.

"Do you look like your father?" Peter asks me.

"No." I shake my head. "I don't look like anyone — just me."

Suddenly I remember about the Saks Fifth Avenue hatbox tucked away on a high shelf in Nana's bedroom closet. It is filled to the brim with family photographs. Looking at old snapshots is a great thing to do on rainy days, but sometimes when I'm sad I like to wade through the brown and white drum-shaped box feeling sorry for myself, and especially for my parents. I stare at their pictures, and they seem so real, as if they were going to walk in the front door any minute. *It was all a mistake*, they would cry, *we're here. For keeps!* But of course, they're not.

Now I want to show the pictures to Peter. "You wait here," I say, jumping off the couch.

"Where are you going?" Pinky calls after me.

"You'll see in a minute. I've got to show Peter something."

"Show me what?" he asks.

"Be patient," I yell from Nana's room.

I drag the wooden stepladder from the corner near the radiator to her closet. Pulling the long string that hangs down from the light bulb, I take a look around. I open the ladder and climb to the fifth and highest step, the way I've done a hundred times before. As I reach for the Saks box, the ladder wobbles.

In that instant a new picture pops into my head. I have tumbled off the ladder and sit in a heap on the closet floor. *Peter!* I cry. He rushes in, takes me in his arms, kisses the tears off my face. Holding my bruised foot delicately, he informs me, *It is fractured.*

The auditions! I weep bitterly.

Tsk. Tsk. He shakes his head. *I'm afraid there will be no audition for you this year, Kate. . . .*

"What's taking so long?" Peter has secured the ladder with his foot. "Hand me the box, Kate, so you don't break your neck," he says. "What's in it?"

"Family pictures," I mutter. "Peter, I have to talk to you."

"You're kidding!" he laughs. "I've known you all these years, and you've never showed off your family pictures . . ."

"I have to talk to you," I repeat. "Have a seat."

Peter climbs the stepladder and we squeeze together on the narrow flat seat at the top. My left arm brushes his right one and I feel little prickles of shyness in my chest. Even that winter day when Peter kissed me I didn't feel this close to him. Now I hope my breath is sweet and the after-shower baby powder pleasing to him.

"This is a weird place to have a talk," he says, resting the big box on his knees.

"What's so weird about sitting in my grandmother's closet with her hundred-year-old heirlooms?" I try to smile.

"When do we get to look at your photos?" he asks.

"You aren't going to want anything to do with me when I tell you what I'm going to tell you," I say quietly.

"This sounds serious," he teases. "Did you rob Bloomingdale's? Take up wrestling? Did you join a new religious movement that has outlawed chocolate chip cookies?"

"I'm not going to audition on the sixteenth." There! I know the words came out of my mouth, but now they seem to ricochet off the closet walls, making hollow sounds in my ears.

Peter doesn't move. In fact, he doesn't seem to breathe.

I pull my knees to my chest, lock my arms tightly around them, and wait.

Nothing.

"Peter?"

I think I hear him sigh, or at least breathe in.

"Tell me you hate me. Tell me I'm a quitter. Say *something!*" I plead.

"I don't hate you." His faraway voice has a fine husky edge and for a minute I think he's going to cry. But that isn't possible.

"The timing isn't right," I tell him. "I'm not ready like you. I know it. My stomach knows it."

"Now I have to audition alone."

I nearly do fall off the stepladder this time. Maybe I didn't hear right. "What did you say?" I ask him.

"I said I'm not thrilled to death to audition alone," he answers in a tone of voice that could never be mistaken for friendly.

Peter afraid to audition without *me?* Impossible! Peter is going to be a star. Everybody knows that. . . .

Now he leaps off the ladder. "Ron will be disappointed." He calmly places the hatbox next to me.

I shrug. "He's already given up on me."

"You still have a couple of days to change your mind."

I shake my head.

Peter turns on his heel. "I've got to get home," he says. Very unfriendly.

I hear the front door close and Pinky's dreadful chromatic scale on the piano. I wish, for goodness sake, Nana would come home. Suddenly I feel exhausted, too tired to move.

When Nana comes in, I am still on the stepladder, and I am crying.

"Kate?"

"I told Peter," I mope.

"It must have been awfully hard," she says.

"He'll never speak to me again."

"He'll speak to you." Her voice is soothing and firm at the same time.

" 'Now I have to audition alone.' That's what he said, Nana."

A slip of a smile. "And now *I'm* beginning to understand," she says slowly.

"Isn't it stupid?" I continue. "Peter is afraid to audition without me!"

"I guess," she winks, "even superstars are entitled to a case of the jitters."

"He sure had me fooled," I comment. "It's a funny thing, Nana, I always thought I knew Peter. I thought I understood everything about him."

"I'm not sure we ever stop learning things about the people we really care for," she answers.

"You're so smart, Nana."

"Let's just say I've been around awhile." She smiles.

"You know," I begin, "there's something I've been wanting to tell you for a long time . . ."

"Mmmhmmmm?"

". . . but there's never a chance around here."

"I'm listening," she says.

"This probably isn't the right time to mention it since I don't even know if Peter and I are talking to each other . . ."

"Yes, Kate?"

I lower my voice to a whisper. "It's just that I sometimes think I'm a little bit in love with Peter."

"I could tell," she answers. Very blasé.

"How could you tell?"

When my grandmother smiles a lot, the tiniest crinkles ripple together near the corner of her eyes.

"Some things you don't have to talk about," she says. "You just *know*."

Then Pinky is standing in the doorway. "What's going on?" she asks. "Why is everyone hanging around in Nana's closet today?"

I spring off the ladder and hold my head high. "We're settling things, Pinky. Just settling things."

14

I am sitting on a park bench across the street from the building that houses the National Ballet School. It is drizzly and cold and my eyes wander from outer space to the wide double doors across from me.

March the sixteenth. From my secret post I watched Peter enter the stark modern building at 10:00, and Ariane Dukowsky at 10:05. A few minutes later two or three others from the academy slipped in—but where are the rest? How come more kids from Ron's classes aren't showing up?

By 11:00 I have eaten my sandwich, and the Granny Smith apple. My stomach churns the way it might if *I* were in there, doing whatever it is those kids are doing to get into the National Ballet School. I'm probably just silly to be sitting out here, but something inside me says to wait. So I wrap my arms around myself—and wait.

There's Peter! He pushes through the heavy doors and I am on my feet, waving excitedly. "Peter!"

He looks around, then spots me. I can tell he is surprised, and it's no wonder. We haven't spoken a word in days, since I told him I wasn't going to audition. Now he crosses Broadway slowly, after waiting for the traffic light to change.

"How did you do?" I ask when he is sitting beside me.

"What are you doing here?"

"Well? How did you do," I repeat, "in *there?*"

He looks puzzled. "You still haven't told me what you're doing sitting around in the rain."

"Maybe I just felt like sitting around in the rain," I answer.

"Sure."

"Well, actually," I begin quietly, "I came to wish you good luck, but then I didn't have the nerve. So I decided to hang around in case you had some nice news to tell me."

"Oh," he gulps. "But I guess it figures."

"What figures?"

"It's just that . . . what I mean is . . . when you do stuff like this, I realize . . . well, I realize what a good friend you are."

"I know it," I say lightly. "You're a lucky guy to have a friend like me."

But Peter doesn't allow himself to smile, even a little. "You didn't audition," he says quietly and without looking at me. "I can't believe you didn't audition."

"Believe it," I answer. "I didn't audition. Anyway, that's no reason to quit talking to me."

"I didn't quit talking to you."

"You've been pouting for days," I say sternly. "Very immature." I'm beginning to like the way I'm able to lecture Peter.

But then he is pushing up the brim of my yellow rain hat. He kisses my cheek. It's all over very fast, yet it's never a bad thing to be kissed by Peter. "Friends?" he says.

"Friends."

All of a sudden Peter's eyes are filling with tears. "I made it," he whispers. "I made the National Ballet School."

"Peter!" I shriek. Then I throw my arms around his neck as if I'll never let go. "Peter!"

We take the bus uptown and get out at Eighty-sixth Street. I treat Peter to a coffee ice cream soda at Jake's and make him tell me everything that goes on at an audition for the National Ballet School. Once he gets going he doesn't stop talking, and I, the captivated audience, hang on every word.

"Who else made it?" I keep asking. "Who else, Peter?"

But he shrugs and insists he doesn't know.

"Let's take class," I say suddenly, tossing a quarter on the counter for the greasy one's tip. "We can make the 1:00 if we hurry."

"Are you kidding?" he exclaims. "I'm wiped out. First I've got to break the news to my father; then I'm going to sleep away the next two days."

"Too bad," I smile. "Ron's class is kid stuff compared to what you'll be doing at the NBS."

Everybody is there today. Everybody. I can't hear myself for all the commotion in the studio. "What's going on?" I try to find out. "What's all the fuss about?"

The word is out. Ariane Dukowsky made the National Ballet School.

A hundred tiny hammers are pounding inside my head. I break into a sweat. And the tears I can't keep from coming are streaming down my face and my neck. I hate Ariane! I knew this would happen. She and Peter are in, and I am out. It's not fair.

I head for the aloneness of the *barre* at the far end of the room and swing my right leg up on it. Leaning toward the knee, I reach past pointed toes with my fingertips. I stretch until it hurts, and then I stretch a little more.

"Why didn't you audition?" The voice behind me is Ron's and it is ice-cold.

I lift my leg off the *barre* and stare ahead, at the dirty white wall where some long-ago person penciled the message "Jane loves Bryan."

"I am disappointed, Kate." I can barely hear Ron for the drumming in my head, and the quiet of his voice. "You had every reason to try." Still, I can't turn to look at him.

"Maybe," my voice is a cracked whisper, "maybe next year."

"Next year!" He laughs maliciously. "And next year you say, 'Maybe next year.' That, my dear, is not the stuff ballerinas are made of."

Then he is gone and I am breathing normally. Ron doesn't believe me. He doesn't understand a girl may just not be ready. Well, that's too bad, Mr. Perfect. That's too, too bad!

But the arms are trembly as I resume my stretch. And I want to shout with all my might, *This cookie doesn't crumble, Ron Vlostic, you wait and see!*

15

May the sixteenth. The weatherman says the sun is bright and as usual I have to take his word for it. Days like this remind me how nice it would be to live in an apartment with a view. Imagine pulling up the window shade on a beautiful spring morning to the splendor of Riverside Park, the Hudson River, the Jersey Palisades!

Mr. Schumacher disappeared long before I got up this morning, and Nana has been racing around in the horrible gray housedress—the one with elephants—for hours. Today, though, even the ugliest dress in the world doesn't stifle her quiet glow. She's trying to act normal, but it's pretty obvious to me that she is bursting at the seams.

"Please, Nana. Try to sit still." Having submitted to a ten-minute beauty treatment, she is edging toward the rim of the bridge chair before the second minute is up. "You know I can't brush your hair if you're jumping all over the place," I scold.

"I'm beautiful enough," she complains in a tone of voice that comes very close to whining.

"You must be patient," I say sternly. "This is a very important day."

"Of course." Her fingers, unused to idleness, fidget on her lap. "Pinky," she calls, "are you ready?"

Pinky spins into the bedroom in the emerald green dress from Macy's. "Well?" She stands at attention. "How do I look?"

"Very nice," I observe, "but your hair needs a barrette."

Pinky pats her curls. "I'm fine," she says dreamily, whooshing past Nana and me. Twisting this way and that, she flirts with herself in the full-length mirror on the closet door.

"You're pretty as a picture," Nana tells the little peacock, "and the image of my Deborah."

"I know," Pinky answers. "I look just like my mother."

Nana stands in the doorway now, her eyes contracting into that faraway, distracted look. "So many years," she whispers. "How could it be that all this time has passed?"

She doesn't expect an answer so I don't struggle for one. I hate it when my grandmother gets all gushy and sentimental because there's nothing to say anyway, and because I need her to be strong and smiling, even a little bossy.

"Before I know it," she is saying, "you girls will be all grown up and going your separate ways."

"I'll never go my own way. Not me," declares Pinky. She wraps her arms around Nana's waist. "I'm only going with you, Nana."

When Pinky says little-girl things like that, I want to warn her that growing up is a pain in the neck, but we all have to do it. One day she'll have to break away from Nana—and I guess I will, too—but I don't have the heart to tell her. After all, she's just a kid. Sometimes I wish I could be nine again. I'm positive life wasn't so complicated when I was nine.

"It's getting late," I say abruptly. "I'd better get dressed."

It's hard to believe the big announcement came only two weeks ago, on a Sunday morning. We were having breakfast—scrambled eggs and toasted bagels, the way we always do on Sunday—when Mr. Schumacher cleared his throat, folded his hands on the table in front of him, and began to twirl his thumbs round and around each other.

"Mrs. Stein and I have something to tell you girls," he said. I heard him suck in his breath, but my eyes were on Nana when he told us, "Your grandmother and I are planning to be married."

You could have warned me! I wanted to scream at her. But I couldn't even mumble what was on the tip of my tongue. *Getting married is for young people, like you and Grampa were, or my parents. . . .*

"What we would like most of all," I heard Mr. Schumacher say, "are your good wishes."

"Will Nana wear a white dress and march down the aisle?" Pinky asked.

"Certainly not." Nana had a smile for Pinky, but her eyes met mine. "Nothing will change," were her quiet words, "only that Mr. Schumacher and I will be legal. And now we will be four again—a family of four."

Something inside me said I knew all along, right from the start, that this would happen. Something else inside me—and it felt strangely grown-up—said this was one of those situations in life I would have to accept. Period.

So I pushed my chair away from the table, hugged Nana, kissed her soft, warm face. When I stood up straight again, a couple of salted tears slid across my nose and onto the tip of my tongue. But that was okay because everyone else was a little weepy too.

"Well, congratulations to all of us!" I said, a little too loudly.

Mr. Schumacher kissed my cheek. "Thank you, Kate."

I pull the jersey jumper over my head. Very pretty, especially with the silky white blouse that buttons in back. Insisting we should each have something new to wear on her wedding day, Nana had raced us down to Thirty-fourth Street last Thursday afternoon. That's how Pinky wound up with the emerald green and why I am wearing the blouse with puffy sleeves.

Nana bought herself a new hat. It's navy blue, like all her hats, with an old-fashioned-looking veil that covers her eyes. I told her it makes her look like Mata Hari. "In the old days," she answered, "everyone wore a hat. It was the style."

Now she bursts into the room crying, "We must hurry!" She is wearing her proper blue suit, the one that appears every fall for the High Holy Days, and the new hat from Macy's.

"You're beautiful," I tell her, "the prettiest bride ever." Her face is flushed and I wonder for a second if she was this pretty the day she married Grampa. "Nana," I say, reaching into my top dresser drawer, "I would be honored if you wore these pearls today. They were my mother's, you know."

Nana stares at the necklace. "Yes," she whispers as I fix the clasp around her neck.

I hug her then, cheek to cheek, shoulder to shoulder. "Don't be sad," I say, gently fingering the cool and luscious beads. "I'm so happy for you, Nana. I'm happy for all of us!" For the first time, I realize it is true.

"Nana! Come quickly!" Pinky calls from the foyer.

"What's wrong?"

Pinky points to the phone but holds the receiver against her belly. "It's Mr. Schumacher. He's at the synagogue and he says we're late!"

I laugh out loud. "Now look who's got a case of the jitters."

"Shhhh." Nana takes the phone from Pinky. "Listen here, Max Schumacher," she says. "Your three best ladies don't intend to disgrace you. Looking beautiful takes time!" She winks at Pinky and me. "Now, don't you let that old rabbi start without us . . ."

Pinky dashes ahead but Nana and I walk slowly. Down 109th Street. I'm trying to set the pace and I don't feel in a particular hurry. One block north on Broadway. After all, Nana will be married to Mr. Schumacher for a long time, so it isn't the worst thing in the world to want her to myself these extra minutes. Across the wide, heavily trafficked avenue we go. The bottom portion of my stomach begins to rumble like the subway underground.

The old brick synagogue with its heavy wooden doors is tucked between two tall apartment houses. For no apparent reason the ancient elevator creaks to a halt on the second floor, then the third. The rabbi's study is on the fourth. Our little wedding party is waiting in the somber foyer.

"Hello!" Mr. Schumacher is tall and quite handsome in his dark lawyer's suit. He takes Nana's hand, something I've never seen him do before, and kisses her cheek. When he realizes we are all watching, he shrugs—a little embarrassed—then smiles, as if to say *Who could blame me?*

"Hi, Kate." Peter steps out from the shadows.

"Peter," I sigh. What a relief to see that cute, familiar face. I nudge his ribs with my elbow and we walk away from the others. "I'm so nervous," I confess, "you'd think *I* was getting married."

"I know what you mean," he says. "I've never been a best man before. I sure hope I remember what to do."

"You'll be fine," I tell him. "Mr. Schumacher knew what he was doing when he asked you."

"Thanks," he smiles. "You look nice today."

Wow! I love it when Peter says things like that. "You're not so bad yourself," I joke. Actually, he is looking more than a little terrific in his blue blazer and gray flannel slacks, but he'd never catch me saying it out loud.

Rabbi Berman comes out of his study. He is grinning and I wonder for a minute if he ever married off a grandmother before. "Are we all here?" he asks. I look around quickly. We are all here, including Mr. Schumacher's two married sons from California.

"Yes," answers Mr. Schumacher. "We are ready."

Nana promised the ceremony would only last twenty minutes. I don't understand Hebrew and I find myself daydreaming during those parts, mostly about the National Ballet School. I'd be a liar if I said I am one hundred percent glad I didn't audition in March. The good thing about my decision was the instant relief I felt knowing I wouldn't have to commit myself to all of it—the audition, the rigors of the school, the total dedication to dance alone. The bad part is I may never get to be a star and that's a shame because I'm sure I would enjoy being rich and famous. Also, I really dread the day that

Peter decides he has more to say to Ariane than to me.

But who knows? Maybe that day won't come so soon. Didn't Peter tell me what a good friend I was? A lot better friend than Ariane Dukowsky could be. Besides, Peter's almost like one of our family. Just the fact that he's here at Nana's wedding proves it. . . .

Nana repeats some Hebrew words. I love the sounds of her other language. They make me feel warm and safe and remind me of the Friday nights. Come to think of it, I must remember to speak to Nana about something after their weekend in the country. I need to know if my mother liked the Friday nights, too, and if my parents made a special fuss for the Sabbath. Suddenly I wonder what they would say if they were here in this room, right now. . . . I have a hunch they'd approve.

Rabbi Berman faces Peter. He makes a signal with his eyes, and Peter pulls the thin gold ring out of his pants pocket. He hands it to Mr. Schumacher. When Mr. Schumacher slips it on Nana's finger everything inside me turns to jelly. I don't mean to cry, just as I don't mean to do a lot of things, but sometimes a girl just can't help herself.

ABOUT THE AUTHOR

Before her two children were born, AMY HEST worked in the children's books departments of several publishing houses, and also as a librarian. She is the author of many popular children's books, including *Pete & Lily*, *Getting Rid of Krista*, *The Mummy Exchange*, and *The Crack-of-Dawn Walkers*. She has recently taken part in the Reading Rainbow Selection program, which featured her picture book *The Purple Coat*.

Great FREE offer just for you!

Join SNEAK PEEKS™!

Do you want to know what's new before anyone else? Do you like to read great books about girls just like you? If you do, then you won't want to miss SNEAK PEEKS™! Be the first of your friends to know what's hot ... When you join SNEAK PEEKS™, we'll send you FREE inside information in the mail about the latest books ... *before they're published!* Plus updates on your favorite series, authors, and exciting new stories filled with friendship and fun ... adventure and mystery ... girlfriends and boyfriends.

It's easy to be a member of SNEAK PEEKS™. Just fill out the coupon below ... and get ready for fun! It's FREE! Don't delay—sign up today!

GOOD NEWS! The five best friends who formed the AGAINST TAFFY SINCLAIR CLUB will be starring in a series all their own.

IT'S NEW. IT'S FUN. IT'S FABULOUS. IT'S THE FABULOUS FIVE!

From Betsy Haynes, the bestselling author of the Taffy Sinclair books, *The Great Mom Swap*, and *The Great Boyfriend Trap*, comes THE FABULOUS FIVE. Follow the adventures of Jana Morgan and the rest of THE FABULOUS FIVE as they begin the new school year in Wakeman Jr. High.

☐ SEVENTH-GRADE RUMORS (Book #1)

The Fabulous Five are filled with anticipation, wondering how they'll fit into their new class at Wakeman Junior High. According to rumors, there's a group of girls called The Fantastic Foursome, whose leader is even prettier than Taffy Sinclair. Will the girls be able to overcome their rivalry to realize that rumors aren't always true? 15625-X $2.75

☐ THE TROUBLE WITH FLIRTING (Book #2)

Melanie Edwards insists that she *isn't* boy crazy. She just can't resist trying out some new flirting tips from a teen magazine on three different boys—her boyfriend from her old school, a boy from her new school, and a very cute eighth-grader! 15633-0 $2.75/$3.25 in Canada

☐ THE POPULARITY TRAP (Book #3)

When Christie Winchell is nominated for class president to run against perfect Melissa McConnell from The Fantastic Foursome, she feels pressure from all sides. Will the sudden appearance of a mystery candidate make her a winner after all? 15634-9 $2.75

HER HONOR, KATIE SHANNON (Book #4)

When Katie Shannon joins Wakeman High's new student court, she faces the difficult job of judging both her friends and foes. On Sale: December 15640-3 $2.75

Watch for a brand new book each and every month!

Book #5 On Sale: January/Book #6 On Sale: February